THE
Golden Band
OF EDDRIS

THE WORLDS OF
THE Golden Band OF EDDRIS

Scarp

Black
Mountains

Valley of Hune

Cavern

Glawth
Castle

Fane

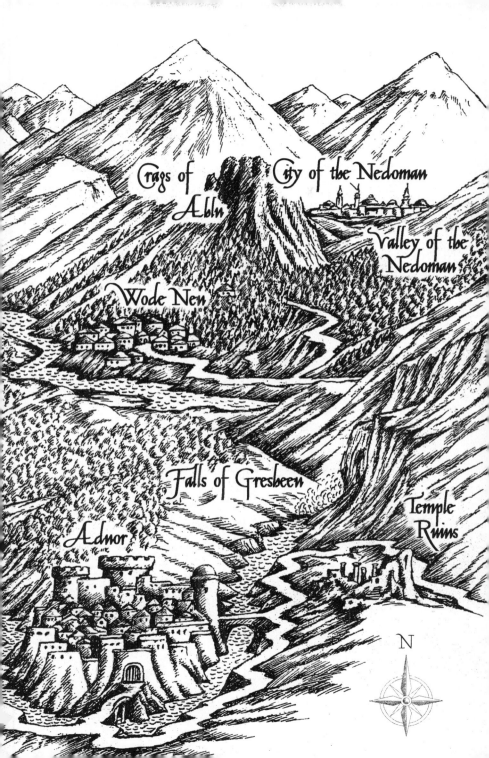

Crags of
Æbln

City of the Nedoman

Valley of the
Nedoman

Wode Nen

Falls of Gresheen

Temple
Ruins

Ædnor

N

To Lee and Jim Patmore with thanks

Henry Holt and Company, Inc.
Publishers since 1866
115 West 18th Street
New York, New York 10011

Published in Canada by Fitzhenry & Whiteside Ltd.,
195 Allstate Parkway, Markham, Ontario L3R 4T8.

Library of Congress Cataloging-in-Publication Data
McKenzie, Ellen Kindt.
The golden band of Eddris / Ellen Kindt McKenzie.
p.   cm.
Summary: When their mother sends Keld and Elylden away, she gives each a special gift to help
them on their journey, and these gifts of power and prophecy aid them when they encounter the
evil witch Eddris.
[1. Brothers and sisters—Fiction.   2. Fantasy.]   I. Title.
PZ7.M478676Go   1998   [Fic]—dc21   97-25583

ISBN 0-8050-4389-6
First Edition—1998
Printed in the United States of America on acid-free paper.   ∞

10   9   8   7   6   5   4   3   2   1

THE
Golden Band
OF EDDRIS

ELLEN KINDT MCKENZIE

HENRY HOLT AND COMPANY   NEW YORK

THE
Golden Band
OF EDDRIS

from them when the sword was seized. The terrible ache of loss still possessed him.

Lips parted, speechless, he turned his head toward his mother. She did not return his look. Her attention was fixed upon the dying fire. Nor did his sister, Elylden, take her eyes from it. She lay with her head in Anna's lap, and Anna stroked the girl's dark hair back from her forehead.

Keld returned his gaze to the smoldering log, the red glow at its center and gray ribbon of smoke twisting from one end. The story tonight was the last of the great legends. Anna would tell none of a later time. He had stopped asking for that long ago. Still numb, the boy leaned forward to lay a few sticks across the embers. To his surprise, Anna spoke again. Softly—as if to herself:

"In that battle Benelf was slain."

"Slain!"

"You never told us!" Elylden sat up, as startled as Keld.

"I am telling you now. As Benelf drew Fel farther and farther from the battle, the enemy hordes, mindless without their leader, became disarrayed. Only for this were the Hundreds able to drive them from the land.

"But no man, however valiant, whatever his strength, could stand alone against Fel. If it was a time for celebration, it was also one for grief. A time of change too had come. The stars had turned. With Benelf's death, the age of the wise ones ended and they departed."

A gust of wind across the chimney bent the flames low

and brought a new puff of smoke swirling into the room. Keld added more wood. Anna went on.

"Up out of the mists of the Valley of Hune they rode, day after day, the Wizards and the Knights of Ahln— kings, lords, knights—brave, strong, and comely beyond all men. With them rode the Women of the Nedoman, courageous, wise, and beautiful beyond all telling.

"Up the mountainside they rode, past the village of Wode Nen. Through the pine forests and over the low rock slopes. Through the wild Wood of Cris Thon and over the high rock slopes to the Crags of Ahln, the watchtowers of the Nedoman. Beneath the Crags the stone gates opened to them, and they passed through into the Valley of the Nedoman. When the last of them had entered the valley, the gates closed."

A shudder passed through Keld that pulled back his shoulders, straightened his spine. That second world—just beyond the Crags of Ahln? "So near?" he whispered.

"Near and yet distant. Here we are of opposites—joyful or sad, kind or cruel—at war with ourselves. There they know what is most precious and cherish it. They are one with each other, with the world, and with the universe— the beloved of the stars. This difference—that distance— is great."

A branch snapped, an ember leaped to the floor. Mindless, Keld brushed it back onto the hearth.

"Histories of the wise ones go no further," Anna said suddenly. "But this is not the end for us. Though Fel was vanquished, he only sleeps. As he sleeps he dreams, and his dreams may waken him. If he walks again . . ." She stopped as abruptly as she had begun.

Keld's stomach tightened. "If he does?" he asked.

"Who can tell the future?" his mother replied, her eye meeting his. She seemed about to add something, but changed her mind.

Keld found himself looking at his mother as if she were a stranger. He had never seen her exactly so by firelight, her face turned half away. If it weren't for the other side of it, she must surely be as beautiful as the Women of the Nedoman. His sister—hers too—a small image of his mother in this shadowed light. What if . . . ?

"Would you ask something?" Anna turned. The perfection vanished.

Confused, Keld shook his head. "No," he murmured and dropped his eyes to his hands.

"I would." Elylden arched her back and stretched her arms. "Why didn't you tell us this before? Who told it to you? Was it your mother? Who told her?"

Elylden! As usual the boy was shocked by his younger sister's presumption. Anna never spoke of her mother or her father, nor had he ever dared ask who his grandparents might be. He always felt Anna would be short with him.

Anna did not reprimand Elylden. "My father told me this," she said. "I don't remember my mother."

"As I never knew my father!" Keld exclaimed.

"Just so." Anna nodded.

"I didn't know mine either," Elylden put in and then, "What was his name? Your father's name?"

Keld drew in his breath.

It was a moment before Anna replied. "His name was Stilthorn."

A prickling of gooseflesh swept over the youth.

Elylden sat up straighter yet and stared at her mother. "The same as the great Wizard? The same name?"

"The same," Anna said quietly. "And now it's time for you to go to bed. There's much to do tomorrow." She rose to her feet, shook her skirt and smoothed it. Then she went to the door and barred it, drew the heavy woven curtains across the high window, and took up a candle to light at the fire.

"Come now."

Elylden stood up. The boy held his hands to the heat. Though it was almost Midsummer Night there was a chill in the air, but he was cold in a way that burning wood could not touch, and he continued to shiver.

"Keld?"

He rose, clenching his jaw to keep his teeth from chattering.

Anna reached out to touch their faces, her usual gesture that said good night. Then she vanished behind the curtain that closed off her small chamber. Elylden moved to the alcove behind the stove. Keld climbed the ladder to the loft.

As he always did, he pushed open the window to look at the night sky.

He saw them coming out of the pine forest above the meadow.

One by one, horsemen in full armor with swords at their sides and spears in their hands. Silver and black under the white moon, they came from beneath the trees to turn south across the meadow behind the cottage. One by one they followed to the road at the end of the meadow. One by one they went up the road to vanish over the top of the knoll.

They made no sound.

The boy watched, scarcely breathing. Once he lifted his eyes to the far mountains. Snow covered, they were often hidden by clouds, but tonight the sky was clear and they glistened cold and hard as pointed blades against the darkness. Against their whiteness rose the black Crags of Ahln. From them a thin rippling line snaked down the bared rock slopes.

It was the stream of riders. There seemed no end of them.

2

He woke to hear the voices of Anna and Elylden below him.

The morning fire was already lighted, the iron griddle hot above it.

"You slept late enough." Elylden pouted as she patted the oatcakes with the back of a spoon. "I had to fetch the water."

The bucket stood inside the door. Keld poured the cold water into the basin and splashed it on his face, rubbing his hands over his eyes and cheeks and mouth.

Anna was beating the sponge of soft dough for bread. The wooden spoon knocked hollow against the sides of the bowl, a sound Keld loved. The boy pushed his hair out of his eyes and slid onto the bench, taking his place at the table.

"You could at least say you're sorry!"

Another day he might have answered his younger sister, telling her it wasn't a load of bricks she'd had to carry, that she'd brought the bucket less than half full. Today he only looked at her, and then his eyes went to Anna's face.

"I was awake in the night," he said.

"Was it the full moon kept your sleep from you? Did you bay at it?" The corner of Anna's mouth pulled up in a rare smile.

"I saw the Knights of Ahln come from the Crags, a line of them, all the way down—as if a giant had drawn on the side of the mountain with the charred trunk of a willow. They came from the woods and crossed the meadow to the road. On and on."

Mouth open, Elylden stared at her brother.

Anna stopped her beating to wipe the sticky dough from the spoon with her finger. "Turn the oatcakes, Elylden. They'll burn."

"Why didn't you call me? Why didn't you wake me?" Elylden cried as she scraped cakes from the griddle.

"I would have but I didn't dare move. They might have seen me at the window. I don't know what they would have done if they had."

"What did they look like?"

"They were knights, I told you, mounted and armed. Some of them carried banners. White with no sign on them. They were like kings the way they rode. I've never seen horses so tall."

"You should have called me! Anna, he should have wakened us! It's not fair! Why didn't *I* see them?"

"You can't see another person's dream," Anna said

dryly. She covered the bowl with the flat tin lid and set it on the brick shelf beside the oven.

"It was no dream," Keld insisted. "I truly saw them coming between the two big pines at the back of the meadow, one at a time. They rode with their heads up, their visors over their faces. They never looked to the side—except one. He turned his head. His visor was up. I could see his face. He looked at the house and pointed his spear at it. At me, I thought, only I don't know. The moon was that bright I might know him if I saw him again." He fell silent, wondering, picturing the half-shadowed face.

"Is that all?" Elylden asked eagerly. "Wasn't there anything more? Did they talk? Did you hear? What did they say?"

"They didn't say anything. They didn't make any sound. Even the horses didn't make a sound. The pines were as still as they've ever been. Their tops were like snow under the moon and so dark below you couldn't see the riders until they came into the meadow." He hesitated. "There was one thing, though."

"What was that?" Elylden was almost jumping from the bench with excitement, the oatcakes forgotten on her plate.

"The air was as cold as winter. I could smell snow. I could smell the Wood of Cris Thon."

Elylden sat back, her hands too heavy to lift from her lap.

Anna set a bowl of clabber and a plate of wild strawberries on the table. "Eat your breakfast. There are chores to do."

They went into the meadow.

"The horses will have left a trail," Keld said.

But there was nothing. Not so much as bent grass, except where the cow had been.

They went through the meadow to the rutted road, up the road and down the other side of the knoll all the way to the spring, but hunt as they would, there was no sign.

Elylden was so disappointed she cried and stamped her feet. She wanted a trace of them so badly she thought of bringing the pony to leave hoofprints in the mud so that her brother might find them. But he would know. Besides, this was too important to pretend.

"Never mind, Elyl," Keld told her. "They were here. If they could go by without making a sound, why should we think they would leave a track? They were here, I know." One corner of his mouth pulled sideways and he scowled. Elylden knew the look. It came when he knew he was right. All the talking in the world would not—could not—make him say otherwise. Comforted, she wiped her sleeve across her nose.

They went back to the meadow—still early, the dew had not yet dried—and into the pine wood that was always cool even on the hottest day. Keld lifted his head.

"There!" he whispered. "Do you smell it? They've left the scent!"

Elylden's nostrils widened. She pressed her lips together

and sniffed, then opened her mouth to draw the air in to taste on the back of her tongue. The peculiar freshness of new snow and the fragrance of air light with wild roses, the sweet-sharp scent of crushed needles of balsam mingled with the ancient mold of rotted leaves, and with yet one more, rare, elusive, that had no other name. Her dark eyes grew darker in her face gone pale.

"The Wood!" she whispered. "The wild Wood of Cris Thon!"

3

nna turned from poking the fire and dusted her hands together. "You've finished your chores? Then listen to me. I've made up my mind. You will leave today as soon as the bread has baked."

Keld stopped rubbing at the dirt on his knuckles.

"I had thought you might leave tomorrow morning, but there is no need to wait."

"Leave?"

"It's time. You will go to the village of Adnor, to a potter there."

"To Adnor?"

"It's little more than a two days' walk beyond the falls of Gresheen. I've made a pack of your clothes." As she talked, Anna brought the bowl to the table and tipped the twice-raised dough onto the board. "It's time you were among others, and Wode Nen is no place for you. If you are to make your way in the world beyond the falls, you must know something other than milking a cow and digging stones from poor soil. You will learn what the potter has to teach you."

"But I don't want . . ."

"Haven't you asked often enough when you might leave this place?"

"Yes, but . . ."

"And what have I always told you?"

Keld's throat tightened so that he could not reply.

"That he would leave when the Knights of Ahln rode down from the Crags," Elylden murmured, her white face showing the startled disbelief Keld felt within.

"So?"

"But I thought . . . and you said it was only a dream!" the boy exclaimed.

"Some things are dreams," Anna said. She cut the dough into three equal parts and folded each upon itself quickly and surely. In a moment there were three round loaves, smooth and firm as piglets. She paused and looked full into Keld's face. "Some are not."

The churning in his mind settled to his stomach. "But what about you and Elylden? Here alone . . ."

"I have looked after you these fifteen years. I can look after myself. As for Elylden, she will go with you."

"Go with me! She's too young! She can only ride the pony, not a horse. She can't fight with a sword!"

"I said nothing of riding horses or fighting with swords. I spoke of a potter. He is a master. Though he is blind, his hands are sure. I learned from him."

Keld could not help but glance at the shelves where not only clay bowls and pots stood, but figures as well, small statues of animals, and the four busts.

Anna went on speaking. "You will learn to use your hands for something other than killing."

"I hadn't thought to kill. Just to fight! Do battle."

"Know that battle means killing. Kill or be killed. If you must, you will, but better to succor than slay."

"But how will I . . . ?"

"Everyone knows him. All you need do when you come to Adnor is ask for the street of the blind potter. Tell him who you are. He knows me. He will give you a place to stay. He will teach you to shape clay. As for Elylden, she is not a baby, and is quite able to look after most of herself. What she can't look after I shall expect you to do."

"Shape clay! Look after Elylden!"

"I can look after all of myself!" Elylden cried at the same moment.

"You are too young to walk alone among strangers." Anna had rubbed the loaves with fat, returned them to the shelf at the side of the oven, and covered them with a cloth. They would rise for the third and last time. "You will stay together at all times. See to it, Keld."

The boy swallowed and nodded. He rubbed his nose in dismay. He wanted to go, yes! But so soon? Today? Beneath the rounded cloth the bread would swell sidewise and upward and then be baked, all in two hours.

Then he must go. But—a potter! Elylden! It was not what he wanted to do!

Anna rinsed her hands and dried them on her apron. She sat down at the table across from them, her one hand flat on the board, the other with fingers curled.

Keld looked into his mother's sighted eye, then looked away. Not because her face bothered him. He was accustomed to the shriveled and scarred side of it, the eyelid that drooped over the white eye, the lip sagging at the corner. He did not turn from that as he knew the villagers did. He turned from the look in her other eye. That sometimes-look that went to the back of his own eyes, traveled around and through the inside of his skull, read all that was there, and finally came to rest on the bones at the nape of his neck.

"For the last time, Keld, spell me the rune of regis arcanum."

Keld sighed. Even though he understood none of it, how could he ever forget? He closed his eyes and recited:

> *First to come, last to serve.*
> *Fire bright over the sea,*
> *White foam and black rock,*
> *Golden fruit of the tree.*
> *Dark water, white mists,*
> *Still rivers in hands of flame,*
> *Shining chain and serpent's coil,*
> *Breath of a forgotten name.*

Cave of ice, nameless wood,
Fortune's stone in circle of dread,
Power wrapped in raven's black,
Shining eye of death's head.
Woodman's axe and blighted land,
Two that are hidden and one that's freed.
Regis arcanum, rex cantorum,
Song of the wind, voice of the reed.
Last to come, first to serve.

Anna nodded, then turned to Elylden. "And you?"

"I know it." Elylden scowled, her dark brows coming together over her even darker eyes. She did not like to repeat it after her brother. She wanted the sound of his voice to stay in her mind. The way he said it sent a shiver from behind her ears to the end of her spine and raised gooseflesh on her legs above her knees. The chill would thaw with the sound of her own voice.

"Repeat it." Anna fixed her eye upon her daughter.

Pouting, Elylden spoke the lines in a hasty monotone, trying not to think of what she said, trying to keep hold of Keld's voice.

When she had finished she looked defiantly at her mother. "I can say it backwards too. 'Evres ot tsrif, emoc ot tsal,' " she began.

A cold breath touched the side of Keld's face.

"Enough!" Anna spoke sharply. "I don't want you to say it backward. Never! There is enough trouble in the world without your bringing more. Never! Do you understand?"

Mother's and daughter's eyes held for a moment. Then Elylden looked down and to the side.

"Never!" Anna repeated.

"Never," Elylden echoed in a low voice.

Anna rose and began setting dishes away. She put the bowl with the rim of dried dough to soak. Her back to the children, she closed her eyes, pressed her lips tightly together, biting the lower one.

"Is there a reason, Anna?" Keld asked.

"For what?" She lifted her head.

"For not saying it backward?"

"Yes."

"Then neither of us will say it backward, will we, Elyl?"

"No. I won't."

Anna let out her breath quietly; her shoulders drooped. Keld! If only . . . No. There was no other way. "Look around. There may be something you want. Make sure. Anything left will have to stay."

She walked with them up the path to the road that was little more than a track. She went up the road with them to the top of the knoll.

"I'll go no farther." Anna put her hand into the pocket of her dress and drew out a handkerchief which she unfolded. "I have this to give you, Keld." She took a ring from the cloth, a gold band with a dark stone set in it.

A sharp pulse ran through his palm as he slipped it on his finger.

"Is it a wizard's ring?" he asked in a whisper.

"No. You are no wizard, Keld. It was your father's, given to him by his father. Wear it always. Give it to no one. It is all the proof you have of who you are, other than your face. But in the world beyond the falls, what of your father lies in your face is not enough. Guard this ring. It will help you find your kin. You must do this."

Look for aunts and uncles and cousins, he told himself in despair. "And make clay pots," he said aloud.

"I said learn to shape clay. There is a difference."

Anna turned to her daughter and put her hands on her shoulders.

"*Your* father left no ring. I have only words for you. Knowledge, like power, sleeps and wakes. You must be aware, alert to all things, no matter how small, so that when there is an awakening you will be ready. Understanding will come. The meaning will be clear to you."

"The meaning of what?" the girl asked.

"That is what you must learn." The woman lifted her hand and touched Elylden's face, then Keld's. A farewell.

Still, she hesitated.

Keld waited for her to speak.

"I don't know what has drawn the Knights from the Crags of Ahln. I fear a great threat, the loss of something priceless. But I doubt you'll see them as you saw them here, in armor and astride their horses. Their task is to defend, but that does not always mean to kill with a sword. What threatens will determine their way. Benelf fought with a sword, but even in war, his last choice was of another kind.

"Remember too the Wizards and the Women of the Nedoman. Their power is as great, if different, from that of the Knights. Respect it.

"As the Knights will do, look to what is needed. Use your mind to understand what speaks to your heart. If you have to use a sword . . . but better to use your hands to create than to destroy. Build with them. Care for your sister. Pay attention to what she tells you."

Suddenly she put her arms around them. "I have given you everything I have," she murmured. The next moment she turned them and gave each a push. "Go now. Make your way. Go," she repeated. "The world is waiting for you."

Brother and sister started down the slope. When Keld stopped to look back, Anna had gone.

4

nna walked swiftly down the hill. She entered the cottage and barred the door behind her. After pulling the curtains across the window, she set about a number of matters quickly and thoroughly, as if every movement of her hands had been planned.

One at a time, she took the four busts of unfired clay from the shelf, blew a sprinkling of dust from each, and brought them to the fireplace. One was of Keld, one of Elylden. The other two were of men, both young, but of quite different appearance. She knelt, set them carefully in the brick oven, and closed the door upon them.

A pack similar to the ones carried by Keld and Elylden was placed in the shed. She took up a pail and went into the meadow. Though it was still early, she milked the cow, then shooed her through the gate to a path between the pine wood and a thick growth of hazel.

"Go on!" Anna held open the gate and slapped the cow on the rump. "He'll be glad enough to find you. He's always had his eye on you. Go on! Hooo!"

The cow ambled to a patch of flowers, looked over her shoulder at Anna, stretched her neck, then lowered her head to graze.

Bucket in hand, the woman returned to the cottage. She poured milk into a bowl for the mother cat. The rest was emptied into a clay bottle, corked, and set in a bucket of cold water.

She led the pony from the shed.

"It's time, Werfyl," she murmured as she harnessed him to the cart.

The pony blew softly and lifted his lip over the handful of oats she offered.

The pack, the jug of milk, and the kittens were placed in the cart. The mother cat jumped in after, stepped into the box, and lay down with her kittens. They mewed and climbed over one another for a privileged place. The slowest of them found himself trapped under a practiced paw and complained at the top of his voice over the prolonged washing of his ears.

Once more Anna entered the cottage. Though it was still daylight, she filled the oil lamp, set it on the table near the window, lighted it, and adjusted the wick. For a last moment she glanced around. Her eye came to the place where the busts had stood. With an exclamation she took from the shelf a small object and dropped it into her pocket. She shook her head, then left the house.

Seating herself in the cart, she took up the reins and shook them. The wheels of the cart bent the grass as they passed over it, but within an hour, unless someone looked closely, the track that led into the pine forest between the pair of tallest trees scarcely showed.

Brother and sister loitered at the spring to search once more for the print of horses' hooves, but the damp earth gave no sign except that of deer and fox. They followed the rutted path up to the mountain meadow, crossed that, and skirted the gray cracked boulders that rose like hunched shoulders above them. They stooped to drink where a second stream rushed clear over the pebbles, then followed the water down to a pool formed above fallen logs. They rested and watched the frogs and minnows in the reedy edges of the pond before crossing over to the deer path on the other side.

Still there was no sign.

Again the climb was steep. Elylden's chattering was broken by longer and longer times of quiet. Her silence left Keld to his own thoughts. The Knights of Ahln . . . they *must* be going to Adnor. That was really why he was going there. Anna did not mean him to be a potter! When he found the Knights, he would find someone to look after Elylden. He would come back for her after . . . what? Oh, surely something more wonderful than rolling coils of clay! The reason they had come down from the Crags—he would join them for that battle. Memory of the early-evening vision came to him, sudden and sharp. The excitement, thrill! Though the grief after . . . He pushed that from his mind. After *this* battle, he would go home to Anna and she would be pleased and proud.

"I'm tired." Elylden's words brought him back from spears, swords, and prancing horses.

"We just rested a minute ago. We have to go on or we'll never get there."

"It's not been a minute. It's been a hundred hours. I won't go any farther." Elylden, her mouth turned down, plopped herself at the side of the road they now followed.

"We can rest a bit." Keld sat beside her. "But Anna told us to stay tonight where the rocks hang across the way."

"I don't know where that is. It's too far."

Keld rummaged in his pack, found the loaf and broke off a piece. "Here. You'll feel better after you've had some bread."

"I'm not hungry."

"I am." He ate the bread and then rose to his feet. "Let's go."

Elylden did not get up. She stared at the ground.

"Come on!" Keld said impatiently. "It's getting late."

She looked up, troubled. Her eyes filled with tears. "I want to go back," she said. "I don't want to go to Adnor to be a potter."

"You aren't to be a potter. I am." Keld scowled.

"But what am I to do?"

"You'll find something. You'll learn something."

"I don't want to. I want to go home!" Suddenly she put her head down on her knees and began to cry.

"You can't, Elyl." Keld spoke with even less patience. Every minute put more distance between him and the Knights. "Anna said you were to come with me. I told her you were too young, but you know what she said. She has her reasons."

"She always has her reasons! She never tells us what they are! I want to go back. I need something and she didn't give me anything."

"What do you mean? What do you need?"

"She gave you a ring. She didn't give me anything!"

"It's my father's ring. Your father didn't leave one. She would have given it to you if he had. You know that."

"I don't mean that. I want something from *her*. It didn't have to be a ring. It could have been a thimble, or . . . a spoon, or anything. I don't know what!" She wailed and sobbed now, crying as Keld had never heard her cry, as if the world were falling to bits around her.

Argue, reason, plead, or threaten, Keld could say nothing to make her stop. "Here," he said at last. "You can wear my ring part of the time. Take it! You can wear it on your thumb."

"No! It's yours." She pushed his hand away. "She said you were never to give it to anyone."

"But you're my sister. It's almost the same."

"Only half a sister," she sobbed.

"It doesn't matter half or whole. You're still my sister."

"You can't give it," she said, her voice trembling, but her crying grew less. She drew short shaking breaths until at last she sighed and again sat staring at her shoes.

"Let's go now," Keld said.

"No."

"Yes! We have to, or we'll never come to Adnor."

"You go. I'm going home."

"You can't go alone! It's hours of walking and I'll not take you back! You're to come with me! Now!"

"No!" Elylden's face, blotched from crying, grew bright red. "I won't!"

"You come with me or I'll . . . I'll . . ." Keld did not know what he would do. He leaned down and put his hands under her arms to pull her to her feet, but Elylden set her weight against him and he could not lift her from the ground. He tugged at her, dragging her down the road, but she dug her heels into the dirt, and after a minute of hauling he gave up. Grinding his teeth, he sat down on a rock and glared at her. Elylden drew her knees up under her chin, wrapped her arms around her shins, stared back at him, and waited.

"Eight years old and acting like a baby! This is wasting time!" he exploded after a minute. "I'm going on. Come with me or sit there by yourself forever!" Keld got up and started walking down the road. At the curve he glanced back. Elylden was watching him. He went on, counting his steps. Two hundred. Two hundred and seven. He stopped and waited for her. She did not come.

So angry he could have cried himself, the boy grated his teeth. If he had to take her home, Adnor and the potter would stay where they were, but the Knights of Ahln would draw farther and farther away. He would never catch up with them! Never ride with them! He took a deep breath and looked across the valley. A curve had brought him around to where he could see the cottage they had left. How small it was, and far away! His shoulders slumped. He turned back.

To his relief, Elylden still sat on the path. She had not moved except to hide her face in her arms. She huddled small and alone with the high mountains behind her and the valley dropping steeply away beside her.

"Get up," Keld said gruffly when he came to her. "I'll take you home."

She lifted her face, so pale and frightened that he was now ashamed of himself as well as being angry.

Elylden shook her head. "No," she said in a voice as small and frightened as she looked. "There's no use. Anna has gone."

"Gone? Where? To Wode Nen?"

"I don't know where. But she'll never come back."

"I don't believe you! Come with me—up ahead there. You can see the cottage. We'll watch. We'll see her."

Elylden rose and followed him. In a few moments they gazed together at the miniature cottage, garden, and meadow so far away.

"You see?" Elylden said. "The cow isn't in the meadow. And the pony is gone. The cat and the kittens are gone too. I know. They're all gone."

Keld stared at his sister and then again at the distant hillside.

"It's almost evening," he protested. "She's brought

the cow into the shed to milk. See? The gate is closed.
She couldn't wander away." But the longer he looked,
the more deserted the place seemed.

"They're gone," Elylden repeated.

Keld did not argue more. All at once he was hollow
from his throat to his knees. Even the crooks of his elbows
felt empty.

Elylden continued to look across the valley, then lifted
her eyes to the Crags of Ahln. Keld's gaze followed hers.

"Where did she go, Elyl?" he whispered. "Why?"

"I'm not sure," his sister said, her eyes still on the
Crags. "Perhaps she means to fetch something for me."

"From there?"

"Maybe. Yes, I think so."

Keld shivered. "Come on, Elyl. It can't be far to the
rocks."

The shadows of the western hills filled the valley. They
fell across the lonely cottage on the mountainside, then
darkened the high meadow. The tops of the pines burned
gold for a moment. The sky flamed and slowly faded. The
fluttering of birds ceased.

For some time the lamp continued to light the window. Then it too grew dim and went out.

Darkness and silence lay upon the cottage and meadow.
The hours passed. The stars marked midnight and moved
on. Two hours. Three.

A branch snapped, a loud crack. The leaves of a bush

trembled though there was no wind. For a minute all grew quiet again. Then came a harsh cry and the rush of feet. Something heavy was thrown against the door. A torch flared, then another and another. In minutes fire leaped all around the cottage and from the roof. Dry sticks were thrown against the walls to feed it. The flames rose high, crackling through the thatch, lifting wisps of burning grass into the air.

"Burn, witch! Burn!" a hoarse voice shouted as the fire burst from the windows and roared to the sky.

5

nna sat up and remained cross-legged, her head bowed, her face in her hands. When she looked up at last, the stars had faded, the sky paled. The cat, the tail of a mouse before her, cleaned her chops and ears. Anna rose and washed her face at the stream.

The cat leaped into the cart, stepped into the box, nosed her kittens, bestowing a lick here and there, and settled among them. Anna harnessed the pony, then suddenly she bowed her head once more, clenched her fists. Elylden . . . Keld . . .

"No," she whispered. "They will be all right. Keld is old enough. The village of Adnor is a good place, the people caring. It has been sixteen years, but the potter will know . . ." She shook the reins.

This was her second journey up the mountain. There was little she remembered of the first, she had been so young. As for the feverish journey down twenty years ago, she had been so filled with terror, so distraught she saw nothing that was not distorted, monstrous.

Pushing that memory away, she turned her thoughts to her senses—the coolness of the breeze, the warmth of the sun, the scent of pine or that of alder, green against blue shadows, the wail of a kitten without its mouth full, the tumble and clack of the cart wheels.

A mass of stone jutting from yellow moss brought a memory of being small and weary and lying against the soft arm and breast of a woman. Dust and the low murmur of voices.

The afternoon of the third day she came to the dark cleft in the rock. She pulled hay from the cart for the pony. Milk for the cat poured thick and sour. Anna shook out her hair, combed and plaited it afresh, wrapping the two long strands twice around her head and pinning them. An image from the morning, the blackened heap of timbers far below, flames and a haze of smoke still lingering, tightened her mouth.

In the darkness of the cleft a second memory came to her—a sudden vision of her smallness as her father took her from other hands, held her close, and, wrapping his cloak tightly around her, bound her to him. Her head lay on his shoulder, his collarbone hard beneath the tip of her ear, his voice deep and resonant as he called to others.

She glanced back. The mother cat lay still but tense and alert, her head up, her yellow eyes watchful. The sleeping kittens pressed close against the mother's side.

"Just so I felt safe," Anna murmured. What had it been for her father and the others to pass through the wood? Had they known fear or were they beyond such shadows?

As a child, had she felt the heart of Stilthorn beat as quickly as her own was doing? "No," she whispered.

Her own fear had come when she came down the mountain to an unknown world. Now I have tasted its joy and its bitterness, she told herself. I have known kindness and love, ill will and grief. I have lost two husbands, faced death by fire—the pain and scarring. I have seen injustice, lying, and cruelty. I have longed for death. Yesterday I sent my children from me. What more is there to lose, and so to fear?

On that journey down, fear had come from the wood. Its scent, its stillness, the shadows that were darker than darkness, the unbearable closeness of suffocating trees. Paths ended in impassable thickets. Brambles and thorns caught her clothes. Frantic, she had turned back.

Anna straightened as she entered the wood. She would learn what lay there that brought such fear. But the path was clear, the wood not of the alarming darkness she had expected in this first boundary between the two worlds.

Did my terror block the way then? There was no answer.

When she came from the forest, the sun was low. Across the meadow, the corner of the cottage eaves showed at the edge of the boulder. She must come to the seven peaks before sunset. She had no time to stop.

Did another shepherd and his wife live there now?

Zar came into the cottage, pulled the door to, and barred it.

His wife looked up. "What is it?"

Zar shook his head, dropped his coat, and dragged a chair to the fire. Before sitting down he filled a mug with hot water from the kettle, added honey and something more from a jug. He hitched the chair a bit closer to the heat and stirred his drink.

Zar had lived most of his life on the mountainside. When he was young he had left this house but found no fortune. Sixteen summers ago he had come back to an empty cottage. He married, tended the sheep, and gardened the stony soil as his father had before him. As his grandfather and his grandfather's father had. Before that, he didn't know.

Life here was what he expected, and he was glad for it. Until tonight, this very evening when . . .

For all the time he'd lived here, he'd never seen such a thing, never heard of such a thing! If there had been such, you'd think the old folk would have told of it. There would be tales and songs. But there was only silence. Except for the warning.

In the week of Midsummer's Eve, stay away from the rocks below the seven peaks.

As a small boy he had stayed away. As a youth he had once gone to hide among the boulders and watch and had seen nothing. He had bragged of his daring to Ronsil Fen, who lived beyond the far stand of aspen. Ronsil had told his ma. Ronsil's ma had told Zar's pa, and though Zar was nearly a man, his pa had whipped him.

"Why?" Zar kept asking. "Why? Why?"

His back was sore for two weeks, but his pa didn't tell him. When he had followed the hound this very evening, he hadn't forgotten the beating, but his pa wasn't here to beat him now.

It was that fool hound's fault. That fool hound had . . .

"What's in you tonight, Zar?" Ila asked. "You've been sitting staring into that fire without a word to me ever since you come in. Have you lost the clack to your tongue?"

"I'm thinking. Can't a man think in his own house?"

"I've nothing against a man thinking in his own house or anywhere else. But it's not your usual way, being out so late and then coming in to sit and scowl and mutter in your drink. Is it the mule?"

"No." Zar frowned. "It's that fool hound."

Ila looked at the dog.

The hound lay with his nose on his paws, his brow wrinkled. He looked from Zar to Ila and back. Then he lifted his head and began to howl. He howled again and again until Zar seized him by the scruff of his neck and dragged him from the house. Let him go up the mountain again if that's what he wanted! Nothing in the world would induce Zar to follow him as he had earlier, follow him and that . . .

But the dog did not go nor would he be quiet. He whined and scratched at the door and finally set to barking so frantically that Ila let him in again. He slunk to his corner and lay down quietly. Only once did he lift his head to look intently toward the door. The hair on his back rose and he snarled, his lips curling back from his fangs.

Zar stared at the door, half-believing the cart and pony and woman and cat would come through the wood and iron of it, appearing shadow to flesh as he had seen them disappear—flesh to shadow—through the solid rock of the seven peaks.

But they didn't, and Ila said, "What's gotten into that dog lately? Is it the full moon? Will he fuss the whole night through as he did last night and the night before? Keep your peace, Ragat!"

At the sharp words, the dog put his head down and stopped growling. Though every now and then through the night they could hear a rumble come from him. Every time he heard it, Zar felt the gooseflesh prickle on his thighs and scalp.

6

They could not have gone through that wall of rock!

Keld stared unbelieving at the massive slab of shining granite rising above him on the left. On his right the descent was as sheer. He looked again at the trampled bracken, the multitude of hoofprints in the mud. Bewildered, he looked around again. This was the first, the only sign of them they had seen. Where had they gone? Had the Knights of Ahln flown into the air?

"We have to go through there." Elylden pointed to a fissure in the cliff at the side of the roaring falls.

"I know!"

Could the horses have passed through so narrow a place? Keld shook his head and took his sister's hand, leading the way into the cleft.

They found themselves on a narrow shelf behind the falls, the booming roar doubly loud. They were immediately drenched by the high-flung spray. Keld could scarcely see by the faint light that came through the curtain of water. He rubbed his sleeve across his eyes and inched forward, testing each step on the slippery ledge before shifting his weight. Elylden's one hand clung to his, the other to his shirt.

When they came from behind the falls at last, they looked upon a tumble of boulders that followed the falls downward like giant stairs. Keld slipped backward down the face of one, clinging to whatever hold his toes and fingers might find, and dropped to the rock below. Elylden followed, slipping and holding until her brother could reach up to grasp her waist and lift her down. So they made their way to where the bank of the swift river stretched level.

"We'll never get up again." Elylden stared toward the top of the falls. Her wet hair clung to her neck, her skirts to her legs.

"Not that way," Keld agreed, pushing his own sopping hair from his forehead. "We'd have to go through the Valley of Hune." The way his father had come!

"Up from the Valley of Hune," Anna told them, "as the Knights of Ahln came—except he rode alone." Up from the silver mist to Wode Nen to marry his mother, then die in the snows of the terrible winter before Keld was born.

Elylden's father had come from the east, a tall, bearded man with eyes as dark as midnight. Keld remembered riding on his back, the beard brushing his hands as he clasped them around his new father's neck. He remembered being lifted to the saddle of a tall horse, the thrill of it and the touch of fear, and how he had thought, I'll do this forever!

Elylden's father had gone away—Keld remembered that day too. He had taken Keld in his arms, tickling his neck with his beard. *Wait for me,* he had said to Anna and kissed her. In that moment it seemed to the boy that the cottage was filled with fire. Somehow a sense of fire always came to him when he thought of the man. He had never come back.

This moment, with the memory of fire came that of the cottage. Elylden had wakened him in the night, and they had watched it burn until the sun came up. He pushed the image away.

"How can we find the Valley of Hune? Besides, we won't go back." Elylden broke into his musing. "There's nothing there."

Keld could hear in her voice that tears were again close.

"It's why she sent us away, Elyl. It's why she went away. She must have known."

Elylden nodded. "She knew. But why did she send us here? There's nothing here either."

"What do you mean? The Knights of Ahln are here! We saw the hoofprints! Anna sent us after them!" He looked up at the rocks. *Could* horses make their way down? *Those* horses could! There must be another sign of them! "Come on, Elyl! We'll find them!"

She followed him slowly. "I mean the air is empty," she said to no one, because he hadn't waited for her to tell him. "So are the rocks and the river. They don't say anything."

In another minute she ran after her brother and took hold of his arm. "There's someone sleeping," she whispered.

Scroot was awakened by his own snoring. He thrust his tongue around his dry gums and teeth, smacked his lips, and rubbed his hand over the stubble on his face. A stone dug into his ribs. Aargh! He grunted, rolled over, and felt for the wineskin. It was empty. With a snort, he threw it and heard the splash as it fell into the stream.

Water! All there was to drink. He groaned. Life had no mercy. It starved you, froze you, wet you, gave you a bed of stones—and left you thirsty. It muddled your plans, tripped you up, betrayed you—and left you thirsty. It snatched your luck from under your nose, dealt you bad cards, weighed the dice against you—and left you thirsty. If he weren't a stoic, a man who could take life as it was handed to him without crying—a thirsty stoic, to be sure—he might cry.

But he was used to life's tricks. He pulled the stone from beneath his ribs and flung it over his back after the wineskin. He expected no gifts from life. Life was hard. A pitiless woman, not a warm, sweet, soft one who'd pull off your boots and rub your back and serve you a hot meal and a full mug and keep you warm on a cold winter's night. No, she was a shrew-wife who nagged you, beat you with a stick, and made you grub for a moldy crust and a half-empty bottle of sour wine.

He sat up, still working his lips over his gums.

"Why are you fishing there?" a voice asked.

Scroot turned his head quickly, scowled, and blinked, squeezing his eyes tightly shut and then opening them wide to stare.

The vision did not vanish.

Was it more of the same? Scroot had a vague recollection of fleeing a parade of writhing creatures, serpents, hobgoblins that glowed like swamp gas, pink dogs with fins of monster fish, their wide-gaping mouths filled with shining fangs. He shuddered and put his hands to his head.

"Go away," he muttered.

"We didn't mean to disturb you . . ."

"But you'll never catch a fish there. You should drop your line in the pool over there."

Scroot opened one eye. The girl was pointing.

"What do you know about fishing?" he growled.

"I know how and I know where. I know how to clean them and cook them too."

"That's true." The youth beside her nodded. "So do I. Anna taught us. Elyl always knows where they are, though I'm better at catching them because I can throw the line farther. I'll show you." The boy leaned down and picked up the line.

"No! No!" Scroot cried. "Not so fast, you two. I'm

attached to that line." He leaned forward, puffing, took up the string where it lay near his foot and followed it to the hole in the toe of his boot. He muttered and grumbled as he poked into the hole with his finger and loosened the loop from his toe. "There. Throw it if you want."

The boy drew the line from the water, turned over a dead branch, and prodded in the leaf mold until he found a suitable bug. He baited the hook and, holding the line loosely, asked, "Where did you say, Elyl?"

The girl pointed. "Where the grass is hanging over the bank, only a little more this way."

The line whirred in the air. Scroot swallowed and shook his head. A peculiar feeling had come over him with the sound, and cold air crept down the back of his neck so that he shivered.

"What's this now?" he mumbled to himself, snorting and straightening. "More chills and shakes?" But the feeling passed and he watched as a few seconds later there was a gleam of silver and a splash. The boy began drawing on the line. In no time a fine trout lay flopping on the ground.

"Try for another, Keld. There're three of us. I'll use your knife," the girl said to Scroot.

Cheeky, Scroot thought, hesitated, then grunted and handed her the knife. She was too small to mean harm, and he could stop her quick enough if she did. Break her arm with a single twist.

Young as she was, she was quick with the gutting and

scaling. The boy too was quick, bringing two more fish to her in as many minutes, then starting a fire with flat stones set in it. The girl finished her chore and waited for the wood to turn to embers before laying the fish on the heated stones.

In no time Scroot was picking his teeth. It had been good. No denying that. Even the water could have been worse. Tasteless, but fresh at least, and not the scum he was sometimes driven to drink in town. He rested his back against a tree and licked his fingers, looking from one to the other of his new companions.

A youth, no more than a boy. Well, almost a man. Hair lying on his head like a pot of gold coins swirling around and around. Scroot licked the fingers of his other hand and prodded for a bit of persistent fish bone caught between his teeth. Gold coins! Ah, what he wouldn't be able to do with a pot of them! His face browned, that boy. He's been a lot in the sun. Made his eyes all the bluer, a skin like that. Blue as the blue glass in Chellie's ring. No, bluer than that. More like the Lady Sirdde's necklace. He had seen it only two days ago when she rode through the streets of Adnor. A gift from Blygen to his new bride. *There* were blue stones to give a man an appetite! He sighed.

The girl, now, no gold in her hair. Black as a crow's wing it was. Nor blue in her eyes. Eyes black as the night, black as . . . ah! Talk of stones and black! What sort of ring is that he's wearing?

"Where do you come from?" Scroot asked abruptly. "This is a far way for a pair the likes of you to be traveling. The road comes from here and there, but it goes nowhere. Are you from Largh's Mill?"

The boy had scooped water from the river and was rubbing his hands together. "No. From near Wode Nen."

"Wode Nen? Never heard of it. Where's that?"

"That way." The boy pointed off toward the mountains. "On the other side of the falls, behind the hills. We've walked more than three days now."

"What do you mean, beyond the falls? There's no way through."

"There's a way," the girl said.

Scroot shifted his eyes to the girl. "None that *I* know."

"If you've not been, you don't know."

Quick mouth, that girl. Needs some taking down. A good beating. "Never been and never heard of," Scroot said slowly. Gold, that ring. Real? If I had it between my teeth I'd know soon enough! What kind of stone? Black as a hole one minute, but when it catches the sun—ehhh! What a flash of red and green and blue and all of them that is! He drew in his breath. Enough to make you blind!

"And where do you go from here?" He picked his teeth with a twig.

"To Adnor. Do you know that place?" The boy shook the water from his hands and wiped them in the grass.

"Adnor. Now Adnor I know. I've been there a few busy times and it's as good a place as any. In fact I'm on my way there myself. Now isn't that a falling together, that we should meet in this place from nowhere and both be on our way to Adnor? Do you hold with chance?"

"What?"

"Do you believe it was chance us meeting here, or do you think we wuz fated?"

"Nothing's by chance."

That girl!

"What did you say your names was? Kel and El?"

"Keld, with a 'd.' "

"My name is Elylden. Only my brother may call me Elyl."

"Elid? Elin? Will you say it again, slow-like?"

"Elylden," the boy said. " 'Lil,' like 'lily,' only 'El-lil-den.' "

Scroot nodded. He would practice that one before he said it again. The look she gave him!

He scratched his arm. "It's another day and a half or a little more to Adnor. I'll go with you on the road so you don't take the turn for Wilp." It was a sudden change of mind for him to return to Adnor. He had left it hurriedly enough and thought not to go back this year or next. But here was reason to go in the *direction* of Adnor. Might there be even more reason for him to show them the way?

Scroot pushed himself to his feet, swung his pack to his shoulder, took a few steps, and lost his balance. He fell against Keld.

"There!" The boy put out his hand to steady the man.

"Thank'ee. Sat on my foot and it's needles up to the knee. Sorry."

"It's no matter. Can you walk on it now?"

"In a minute." Scroot shook his foot in the air, holding to Keld's arm. No pouch here, he thought. Would the girl carry it? She's a good bit younger. Why might the boy trust her? Or would it be to throw honest folk off? A chit of a girl hiding it in her skirts somewhere! He'd have it soon enough!

"We'll be glad for your help. We've never been there."

Scroot nodded. A peasant boy as innocent as the morning and trusting of whoever! Either he'll die young or the spirits'll protect him forever. The girl now, you could see the suspicion in her face. Those eyes, so dark you can't tell the center from the edge.

Women! What one is trusting? What one can you trust? For sure you never can trust them to lie about the right things. Lie about their ages, they would, or their husbands. But anything important and you're over the coals. He wouldn't be on the spit as he was if it hadn't been for a woman he'd trusted to lie for him and she hadn't! And this one—she was edgewise as a razor. He'd not trust her! Oh, no. Where do you suppose she keeps the money hid?

"Have you the means to pay your way at an inn? You'll need a place to sleep."

"We've no money. We'll sleep on the ground."

"You need a few pennies between you to buy bread."

The boy shook his head. "We brought bread from home. It's gone now. That's why we asked to fish. If the road follows the stream and you lend us your line again . . ."

"How will you fare in Adnor with no money? You can't sleep in the streets without being murdered or thrown in prison, which is the same. It's no town for begging." No money, but a ring like that?

"We'd not think of begging! We're to find work."

"Work!" Scroot spat the word from his mouth as if to clear it of a bad taste. "Well, every man to his way."

"We've someone to find. He'll give us work."

"Hmmp! Work!"

Scroot changed the talk to other things. The day passed. They fished again, with the same luck as before. How was it the girl knew where the fish would bite? Luck. Just luck. Like everything else in life. Well, and these two were luck for Scroot. For there might be no money, but there was the ring. He'd have it off the boy tonight while he slept—no, tomorrow night. They'd fish for him tomorrow. Tomorrow midnight he'd be off with the ring to Wilp. It was plain the boy didn't mean to sell it, and what other use was there for such a gewgaw but to sell it and have the good things the price would bring?

Scroot licked his lips. Thirsty! And no water, fresh or brackish, would slake such a thirst!

lylden was wakeful. Even the night sky and the stars had nothing to tell her about this man with the pocked, whisker-stubbled face.

I'll have to find out because Keld doesn't worry about him, she told herself. *I don't like the way he thinks about me, this man. He doesn't believe I know where the fish are. I always know. Was my father a fisherman?* She tried to imagine her father casting a net.

She had never seen the ocean except as Anna did when she sang of the waves white with foam. Anna knew the sea. Anna knew the deep forests. She knew the gentle hills and the fierce mountains. She sang of them all and her eye would look through the wall of the cottage and Elylden would look through the wall with her.

The girl stared through the tree branches at the bright stars. A week ago she lay with her head in Anna's lap and looked into the fire. The flames vanished. Gray waves broke and ran across the sand. Farther on, they rose to shatter to a froth against rocky cliffs.

First was the time of the ancient ones when no time was measured. When the sea cast great boulders against the shores and ground both rock and cliffs to sand. When the earth opened, and mountains rose, and fire leaped from peak to peak. When the wind howled and scoured the land, joining fire and sea and rock, all four in one.

The sun rose and set, and the stars and moon followed, but there were none who measured days or years, for what did sea or earth or flame or wind care for time? What did they know of good or evil? They only were. But they ever will be. Remember them. The ancient ones.

The first of Anna's legends . . .

There were people too. When Anna talked of the sea, the girl saw them. Naked, their ivory bodies shadowed pale blue and green, they rode from the waves on white horses. She had also seen them coming from the dim silence of the forests, their skins dark, tawny, fair, or copper-colored—dressed in scarlet, gold, and green, people of such beauty and strength as she had never seen in the village of Wode Nen.

The people of Wode Nen hadn't liked her or Keld or Anna.

Would the ones in Adnor be beautiful? Would they like her?

Troubled, Elylden bit her lip. Would she be able to see through the walls in Adnor without Anna there to help her?

★   ★   ★

In the morning Elylden walked close to her brother. This country was still hollow. She slipped her hand into his. He held it loosely. As usual he was thinking about whatever he thought when he didn't notice anything else—like that man, Scroot.

Scroot—what a horrid name. Like scratching your fingernails across gray stone. She hated the way he looked at her brother. She watched his eyes slip sideways once again to look at Keld. He was planning some harm. There was something wrong with a country—having a man like that.

They followed the river through meadows and woods. There was no sign of hamlet or farm or folk of any kind until they came from a thick wood into an opening large enough to hold a village. Something had once been there, for in the center of the clearing was a wide circle of stone with broken columns rising from its edges and steps all around it. Chunks of dark green metal lay scattered in the weeds. Over there grass pushed between charred wooden beams.

"What place is this?" Keld asked.

"No place now," Scroot said as he sat down on the steps. "Blygen and his like saw to that ten, fifty, or maybe a hundred years ago. Who can say? I've heard they did others the same. We'll stay here tonight. Tomorrow'll bring us to Adnor." He pulled a wisp of grass from a crack in the stone and chewed on it. "Go do your fishing or you won't eat."

"You have the line," Keld told him.

Scroot grunted and tossed it to the boy.

Elylden wanted to kick the man from the steps. He didn't belong here. This place had nothing to do with him. It had to do with what had gone from the air.

Slowly she mounted the steps. The sun was low and the stone took on a golden cast. She caressed the smooth surface of a column. Where it was not pitted by the weather it was hard and soft at the same time, sleek and shining as Anna's hair. Much of the cracked floor was swept clear and scoured by the wind, but all around the raised edge, sand, dry leaves, and twigs had gathered to form a mulch from which grass and weeds had sprung up.

The girl walked to the center of the ruin. Her hands felt strangely heavy and her heart beat quickly. The sun was lower now and the few clouds above it turned crimson. Like fire, they were, lying on the hilltops, as if the whole world were flaming.

Suddenly the hills went barren and brown. No tree or bush or blade of grass grew on them. As quickly, the water of the calm river grew to a torrent. Wind whistled through the stone columns and blew against her face, now hot and stinging with sand, now cold with the sharp cut of ice. It wailed and keened and then was gone.

The old ones! Elylden's skin burned.

"Why are you gawking? Show your brother where to fish!" The man's voice broke the spell. All was as it had been a moment ago.

Scroot, sitting there, was driving them even farther! She grew hot with anger, and then the feeling passed.

Scroot would go away. He would die. Everyone like him would die, and then the ones who belonged here would come back.

Comforted, she went down the steps well beyond the man's reach and joined her brother on the riverbank. The line whirred from his hand and dropped into the water.

Elylden woke. The stars hung bright above the roofless temple. A breeze moved through the trees. In it she heard the shuffling whisper of many feet, the rustling of moving beings, voices speaking, laughter, and a distant chant, music swelling, then fading to something sad, something lonely that brought a grieving sorrow to her.

"They were mine," she whispered. "But they're gone now. They've been forgotten. There's no one to talk to them or listen to them."

Who were they? Who drove them away? The music stopped suddenly. There came a single voice. A warning.

She sat up.

"You'd better not take it," she said sharply.

The moving shadow froze.

"If you do," Elylden went on, "you will have your right hand cut off, your eyes put out, and your tongue nailed to the gallows before you're hanged."

"I thought you were a sweet child!" Scroot's voice

came through the dark. "To think such things, let alone say them!"

"I don't care if you think I am sweet or if I'm not sweet. But I'm telling you the truth. If you take his ring, that's what will happen."

Scroot cleared his throat and slouched back on his heels. "And if I don't, will I have a reward for that, Miss Know-all?"

"I can't see that. You'll be hungry and . . . and you'll complain. That's all I know."

"I'm hungry now, as a matter of fact. And cold too and you're a nosy brat. I'll sell the ring and bring food back for you."

"No you won't."

Scroot leaned away from the sleeping Keld.

"If you want gold, you'll have to work for it," she said.

"Aarrrgh!" He fumbled at his belt for his knife.

"I cleaned the fish with it. I still have it."

He turned to stare at the blade that gleamed in the girl's hand. Small as she was, nothing had ever looked more threatening. Scroot's heart gave a lurch, and he crept back to where he had been lying and sat down. The girl watched him but said nothing more. After a while Scroot lay down, wrapped his arms across his chest, and tucked his hands into his armpits to keep them warm.

Elylden lay down and again looked through the branches into the night sky. She wondered how such thoughts came to her. Never had she heard of such terri-

ble things happening to anyone. Never had she seen a gallows. How had she known it was a gallows when she saw
him there?

Would the people of Adnor be like Scroot? Would
they give her such thoughts? She felt hot, then shivered.
Tomorrow they would walk and walk and come to
Adnor where . . . The saliva ran suddenly in her mouth.
She pressed her lips together.

Keld? Anna? Where are you? Anna, I want you!
Please . . .

But Keld slept and Anna was far away. The next
minute Elylden was thirsty. She waited until Scroot began
to snore and then crept past the ruined temple to the river
to scoop up water and drink. And drink.

8

A thirst for knowledge! She had forgotten how keen the desire was to understand, to search out all the secret ways of existence and delight in the wonder of it.

Anna turned to unharness Werfyl, but the reins melted in her hand. The cart crumbled to dust. The pony wandered off to graze in the high meadow. The cat remained crouched in the box on the ground. When Anna bent to touch her, the cat laid back her ears and spat.

"I should have known better than to bring you. There, the way will be open for still a minute." Anna gestured.

Taking up a kitten in her mouth, the mother cat stepped from the box and carried her kitten through the wall. Back she came. One after the other she carried away until only one was left. Before taking that one, she came to Anna, rubbed around and between her legs, then took up the last kitten, went into the wall, and did not return.

"Teach them well, Pelaur," Anna murmured as the

wooden box crumpled and curled in upon itself like parchment consumed by fire.

Anna's eye moved down the mountain to the vast expanse of arid wilderness, a gray barren floor with long upthrust ridges of brown, black, yellow, and red exposed by harsh, driving winds and stinging sand.

To the east the faint blue line of the mountains of Engist were sketched upon the sky. Rising higher northward, they would meet mountains of immense height, peaks rarely clear of frozen mists. Anna had seen them only once, silent, gray, black and slate-blue rock, white-topped against a cerulean sky.

Stilthorn had gestured toward them. *What Wizard, what Woman of the Nedoman, what Knight of Ahln would want to live surrounded by the bland comfort of a plot of mowed grass and a clipped bush? Rather a single flower in the desert, a spire of stone in a cave, a tuft of fox fur in a thorn bush, or these—the old ones. Remember their strength, their eternity, my Teyapherendana. They keep you humbled.*

Humbled she now was as she faced the naked bones of this world that stretched so far. She must cross all of it, and more.

Why had she remembered the valley as gentle? Its variety was infinite, its time unmeasured—that is, if you were a Wizard, or a Knight, or a Woman of the Nedoman. If you were mortal . . .

"What am I now?" Anna's right hand moved over the crippled fingers of her left. Only by going forward would she find if the crossing would be as a swift dream or a time to die. She began the descent.

The vastness of the desert dwarfed her. The wind blew hot, the dazzling sun glared. But, as rippled dunes, shimmering expanses of salt beds, sculptured canyons surrounded her, Anna's perception sharpened. The sight, sound, and taste of change—bluffs cut through by foaming rivers, the roar of waterfalls, a sea of black waves breaking, frothing silver, glaciers sweeping down from mountains ending in cliffs of blue ice, splitting off with a crack like thunder, the silence of giant trees, plains, lakes, brooks purling over colored stones—came swiftly.

Now the vision of the City of the Nedoman, a glow against the deep blue of the mountains. A city of crystal and white marble, of domes, spires, towers, temples, the dwelling place of the Knights of Ahln, the Women of the Nedoman, the Wizards.

The setting sun touched the towers with gold, then pink, then red that deepened. In moments turrets, spires, and domes stood like pale ghosts, their color lost to the violet dusk. As darkness grew, the full moon rose, casting all into light and shadow, turning all to black and silver.

"I am still of it!" she whispered. "I have crossed a world. The sun has set twice in the same day. The moon is again full."

The gardens around the city were as familiar as if she had stepped through the gates of Ahln for only a moment. Wide lawns interspersed with clumps of trees and patches of meadow spread silver-gray to the dark edge of the forests. Pools, mirrored stars. Statues cast soft moon shadows on the grass. The scent of flowers intoxicated.

Anna paused. What . . . ? But it was gone. So fleeting she must have been mistaken. In the Valley of the Nedoman there had never been that breath of decay she had learned of beyond those craggy walls.

But there! She bent to pull a clump of coarse-leafed burr from a flower bed. Carelessness? The statue of Afandia—Anna paused to savor her pleasure, then looked more closely. A chip? The entire side of the hand was gone! Never before . . .

Something was wrong. She grew still. There was nothing. Yes, nothing! An emptiness of the air and of every other presence!

More disturbed her. A rough place in the polished wood of a bridge rail left a splinter in her hand. Scum floated at the edge of the water among the growth of reeds. The statue of Arolestis—the left shoulder cracked and green mold at the base.

"A thousand years did none of this! I have been gone only twenty!"

But ahead of her the vast collection of sloping roofs, domes, spires, and towers, simple yet graceful, showed only perfection.

When she passed beneath the first stone arch there was a rippling along her arms and down her body. The rough homespun she wore quivered as if the threads possessed life. She found herself clad in the shimmering wrap of the Nedoman, radiant, light. Her hand rose to her face to feel the old harshness of skin, the same downward pull of her lips at the corner of her mouth, the same droop of her eye.

Why one and not the other?

She mounted the marble steps to cross the wide temenos with its shining stone and tile and came to the domed court. Marble-columned passages led to the libraries and studies of the great Wizards. Pushing aside the aching desire to greet her father, she entered the fane.

And still there was no one.

Anna's heart was beating too quickly. The palms of her hands were damp, her fingertips cold. "That I should know fear in this place is a flaw in me," she whispered.

At the opposite end of the temple loomed the shadowed archway.

The torquous passage to the groandiformd hall of Eddris—words she had invented and said only to herself when she sat at her father's side and peeked at the low-arched door that led into darkness. Was it for such thoughts she had been sent away? How do you stop the thoughts of children, even if you are Eddris? Why do you punish their innocence, especially if you are Eddris? Why do you deny their truth . . . She stopped her thoughts.

Beyond the entrance the long passage led into the mountain. Only the pale stone of the floor against the dark edges of the walls showed the way. She did not know the time or distance she walked until she discerned light. It came from two torches set on either side of a massive bronze door, the face of it crossed with a strange mingling of iron bars and figures wrought in gold.

Anna would raise both arms to touch a golden spiral, but it was only her right arm, fingers outspread, that she could lift. Her left arm rose only from the elbow, the fingers remaining clawlike, crippled and shriveled. She curled the fingers of her right hand to her palm and slowly lowered her arm. *Eddris knows I am here.*

"Anna! Anna!" Elylden cried out in terror.

"What is it?" Keld crawled on his knees to his sister. "Wake up! You were dreaming!" He shook her. "What was it?"

She sat up and threw her arms around him. "I don't know! Something . . . something . . . a door . . . Anna . . ." Though her terror remained, the reason for it had vanished.

"Anna's all right. She told us she can look after herself."

"I know."

The boy felt Scroot's eyes upon them. He looked over Elylden's head at the man. "She misses her mother."

Scroot shrugged, turned away and lay down. Keld continued to hold Elylden until she stopped trembling. "Can you sleep now?" he asked.

"No."

He looked at the stars. "It's almost morning. I'll lie close."

"She shouldn't go in there," Elylden said in a small

voice. She lay down, pressed her back against her brother's, and drew her knees up to her chin.

The doors swung open silently.

Anna stepped into a vast cavern. Lighted by a thousand torches, a throne carved of the glittering stone of the mountain rose high. Before the throne lay a circular pool. Dark as the empty eye of a skull, the water's surface reflected no light. Instead a shadow rose from it to fall across the throne.

Anna approached the edge of the black pool and gazed across it.

"So you stand before me once more." The voice was sibilant.

Even as she replied, "As I was bidden," Anna knew that it was not in the Wood of Cris Thon but in this cavern where lay the heart of her fear.

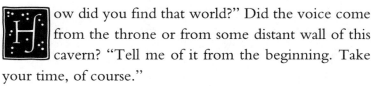

9

ow did you find that world?" Did the voice come from the throne or from some distant wall of this cavern? "Tell me of it from the beginning. Take your time, of course."

Was there a touch of sarcasm in the voice? Impossible for one as great as Eddris! Yet Anna would choose carefully what she said.

"I was given shelter by an old shepherd and his wife."

What did that tell of her seeing the Crags of the Nedoman behind her? She had been chilled and then sick. Weak and shaking, she had crept to the sun-warmed boulders and lain against them until the ache and nausea passed.

How young she had been—not yet as old as Keld—and how terrified, a feeling new to her. Her body was strangely heavy, the air she breathed harsh and bitter. The mountains threatened, the sky was indifferent. How often did she stumble and fall? How she had clung in her fear to that vestige of power Eddris had permitted her to retain!

"I stayed with them for two years. They taught me their ways."

What did that say of scrubbing and washing, milking goats, churning butter and setting cheese, carding wool, spinning, weaving—of the soreness of her hands and fingers, the pain in her shoulders? She had grown used to it. The old man and his wife worked as hard. They had been good to her. She had come to love them.

"By what name did they call you?"

"Anna."

"Did you not tell them your real name?"

"I told them. It was too long. They took the last of it."

What is your name, child?

Teyapherendana.

What did you say? Anna? We shall call you Annie. What were you doing on the mountain, Annie, at this time of night in such a storm? Nay, Jarold, let the child be. She's sick with cold and fright.

"Of course. And after two years?"

"The old man died, and I went with his wife to her brother, a craftsman in a village. There I learned to make pots of clay."

It is not just a vessel you make but a thing of beauty. Though I cannot see it, I can feel the shape, the smoothness, the grace.

The clay had dried her hands but had put in them a desire to shape things other than bowls. *Oh, Annie, you have made the likeness of my Jarold! I'll keep it by me forever and not feel so lonely! There's magic in your hands, Annie!*

"Here too people were kind. After two years there, I

came to the village of Wode Nen where I remained for sixteen years to watch for the Knights of Ahln. You had so bidden me."

"Did you see them?"

"No. I heard of their coming."

There was a sudden movement of a jewel-covered hand, the shimmering ripple of a mantle that showed now gold, now green, now blue.

"Then something threatens. What have you brought to us? In sixteen years you must have done other than watch."

How might she calm herself? Upon a pedestal beside the throne lay a circlet of gold, Eddris's symbol of perfection. It gleamed beneath a lamp. For some puzzling reason, it distressed her. She must find her own. A drop of water on a leaflet, clear, sparkling.

"I left my few possessions behind. I bring my experience."

"Is that all?" Had the voice become sharp?

Anna closed her eyes. The droplet hung in her mind's vision. "What else I had would be of no use here."

"Your grief? Your loneliness?"

If she knew of it, why did she ask? Anna looked again upon the golden band. No, she must keep her eye from that.

"You are right," the voice went on. "Worldly sentiments have no place here. Yours will fade." Again the sleeve rippled gold and green.

"I do not want them to fade."

"Would you keep your pain?"

"No. I ask that I be allowed to return to that world."

"Curious." Then, "Tell me what you did for sixteen years."

Anna's stillness grew. Perhaps Eddris did not know all.

"Well?"

"I married. My husband died before I bore his son. Five years later I married again. By that marriage I have a daughter."

"And your second husband? Did you leave him to come here?"

"He left me. I waited for his return until two days ago."

"You are brief! Sixteen years in half a minute! Your face, why is it scarred, your hand crippled? I am surprised a man would have you."

"It happened afterwards. There was a fire."

"Tell me of it."

A spark of anger flickered in Anna, then died. She saw eyes gleam in the shadowed face beneath the hood.

"They would burn me as a witch."

"You showed them your power?"

"They felt it."

"Why did they only half succeed?"

"The fire would not burn."

"Fire was always partial to you. Still, fire will burn!"

"The fire was quenched."

"How did that happen?"

A mist came over Anna's thoughts. *How did it happen?*

What did Eddris want to know? A light glowed at the center of the tiny drop of water, turned gold, rounded to form a perfect, tiny circle. Her mind clearing, she spoke quietly. "The wind brought rain. Mud and rock slipped down the mountainside. They took it as a sign."

"Superstition! They wanted you dead. They did not try again?"

A sudden horrifying thought—did Eddris want her dead? Then old Pareth's voice. *We'll have the care of you, Annie, and your Keld and your new baby.* He and his daughter had taken care of her. Then Alida married. Last week Pareth died. Three nights ago they tried again.

"Your children—are they still alive?"

"Yes."

"But you left them."

"I sent them away."

Again the hand moved impatiently. "You did not leave them with nothing. What were your gifts to them? Your son, first."

Anna breathed slowly. Her voice must not tremble. "I gave him the quality to love as his father and I loved one another."

"What else?"

"I gave him the compassion, the love his father bore for all of the world, and his courage to defend it."

"And the third?"

"I gave him the gift of knowledge of kin—that he might find his father's people and know them."

"Harmless enough. Who was his father?"

Anna raised her head. "His father's grandfather was the son of Benelf of the Hundreds."

The questioner moved her hand in a gesture of dismissal. "As worthy a one, I suppose, as might be found there."

This was not the moment for anger, yet Anna clenched her hands together so tightly the bones of her fingers hurt.

"And your daughter?" The probing voice continued. "Who was her father?"

"His name was Ericoth."

"That is only a name. Who was he?"

"That was all I knew of him. He came from the village of Eneth."

The questioner was silent for a moment. Then she said coldly, "There is no such village."

"I knew only the villages of Wode Nen and of the potter. Eneth was the name he gave me."

The hand moved for a fifth time. The rings flashed.

"And what did you give her, your daughter?"

"I gave her the quality to love as her father and I loved."

"What else?"

"I gave her my beauty."

"Marred, of course, by her humanity."

Again Anna fought her anger—anger left to her from man's world!

Bracelets shone upon her arm as Eddris reached out to touch the golden band. A sudden coldness passed over

Anna's face, the scarred side of her body, and her shriveled arm as if ice water had been poured over her. In that instant her vision grew sharper. She saw how the light of the torches was swallowed in the cavern's great height and depth. The figure of Eddris grew clear. She looked down at the smoothed skin of her left hand and curled and uncurled the fingers into her palm without effort or pain.

"What else did you give her?" Eddris asked.

Anna passed her fingers over the soft corner of her lips. "Why did you do this?"

"Such imperfection is not acceptable."

"It protected me there!"

"You do not need protection here. What else did you give her?"

"I do not wish to stay here!"

"What else did you give her?"

Anna struggled to keep from answering this implacable voice.

"The third! Why do you not answer me?"

Anna closed her eyes and pressed her hands against them. There was no denying the persistent question.

"I gave her my power!"

The hiss of a serpent filled the cavern, the sibilance coming from all directions, growing louder, then dying away. Into the quiet came the whispered words of Eddris.

"You . . . gave . . . her . . . your . . . power! Why?"

Anna answered in a whisper not unlike that of Eddris.

"Because she is my daughter!"

"You had no right!"

"I had every right!" How was it possible that Eddris was angry? That she had not married, not born a child, was her choice. But how could she not understand what a child meant? "You sent me into that world unknowing, ignorant, young!" Once more Anna fought to grow calm. "I was not told what was expected of me. Nor did I know what I would meet. I could not be there as I was—as I am here. I was human in every way but one. That one way I must conceal for twenty years if I were to live. I came very near losing my life.

"You have asked me many questions. Now I would ask you. What deed was I sent to accomplish? Why did you say to me 'Return when the Knights of Ahln come down from the gates of the Nedoman on the third night *after* a Midsummer's Eve?' Were you mistaken? The Knights of Ahln came down from the gates of the Nedoman three nights *before* Midsummer's Eve! The way would have been closed to me six days later! What barrier was put between them and me that I would not know?"

A silence, then the voice, cold, detached. "It is not for you to question me. What does your daughter know of her power? Where is she?"

Anna did not reply.

"No matter. I will find her easily enough. You will have sent her where you left some trace of yourself. I will seek her where all has become most corrupt. She must be destroyed before destruction is brought upon others."

"No! She will destroy no one."

"She must be destroyed. Your son too. I do not trust his being. They are the threat. Because of them the Knights of Ahln have left this valley."

"No!" Even as Anna cried out, the figure upon the throne began to fade, grow transparent.

"No!" Anna cried again.

There was no answer. The throne was empty. One by one the torches went out until there was no light but that from the lamp above the band of gold.

"No!" She moved swiftly around the black pool to the empty throne, mounted the steps and took up the golden circlet.

"You shall not destroy them!"

The next moment Anna passed through the iron-bound doors, the golden band of Eddris gleaming in her hand.

10

nna hurried through the passageways. She must speak with her father. As in the garden, she met no one. Why? Her heart beating quickly, she lifted her hand to knock at the door of his study.

What if the room was empty?

Even as she hesitated, she heard his voice.

"Come in, my Teyapherendana! What is troubling you?"

Trembling, she pushed open the door.

Stilthorn rose from his chair and came toward her. His arms were around her and she felt the strength, the power, the comfort, and the peace that came from him just as it had when she was a child.

"Why do you weep? I should think you would be rejoicing! The honor is great, and you are deserving of it."

He stepped back, took her face between his hands, and looked into her eyes. His smile faded, and his expression grew more and more grave.

"What has happened? What has Eddris told you this morning?"

"This morning!"

"Since you left me, of course. Tell me," he ordered. "Quickly!"

The old way—she knew it well—not with words, but mind to mind, thought as swift as the passage of light.

"Why did she do this? What reason . . . I don't understand!"

"Don't you believe me?" Anna asked.

He looked startled. "Why shouldn't I believe you?"

Again Anna felt tears come to her eyes. "It has been so long I've forgotten what trust was. In man—there is suspicion, deceit, injustice!"

"Is that all?"

"No. There is kindness and love, courage and devotion."

"Man is man. Made of opposites. No, I do not doubt you. It is Eddris, an admirable woman in every way— strong, intelligent, beautiful—she was chosen for those qualities until you should come of age."

"Why until I should come of age?" Anna asked.

"The place she held had been your mother's. If you were worthy, it was yours as soon as you were old enough to understand. This morning when you went to her—this morning, you say twenty of man's years ago?" He again took her face in his hands, shook his head. "There is no sign of such time passing . . . except, perhaps, a trace in your eyes."

"I have lived that time!" Anna cried. "I have . . ."

"I know," Stilthorn said softly. "It is Eddris' perfidy—to

hide from us what she did. I don't know . . . outwardly . . .
yes, it is hard to see. But she could not take your memory!
This morning she was to tell you of your future. To
entrust you with the sources of all the knowledge that the
Women of the Nedoman possess. To teach you . . ."

"She told me nothing of this," Anna whispered. "She
said I was unworthy to live here. She diminished my
power and sent me away."

"So you have told me. And you have suffered long,
while those years of man's were scarcely an hour to me."

Anna put her hand to her lips. "Time," she whispered.

"This corruption of Eddris', this infamy—I would talk
with the Wizards, Knights, Women . . . What do you
mean, time?"

"I came through the Valley of Hune to come to
Wode Nen!"

"How else would you have come?"

"I lingered there!"

"Why? How long?"

"Because . . . we lingered, and I don't know how long!
Days of the Nedoman, perhaps . . . weeks. Twenty years
of man—and here still the same morning! There—a
hundred years? Two hundred? Who can say? Keld, Elylden . . . what have I sent them into? It can't be as it was!"

"You will find no Knights to talk with, Stilthorn. They
have gone. Eddris too has left—to destroy my children! I
know where they are. I shall go at once, find them before
she does. I will protect them! I have this!" Anna held out
her hand to show him the golden band.

Again the Wizard was startled. "The Knights have left? With no word? They would go to that world only when they sensed a terrible need to come, a menace . . . Where did you get *that*?"

"What need? My children are no threat! Eddris told me to watch for the Knights before I left here—before they were born! She *sent* the Knights. This is her golden band. I will take her power with me."

"Of course your children are no threat! What are you saying about the Knights? To know when they will be needed is part of their being! Eddris has no sway over them! Nor can you use her power. It is her place that is yours. That is what you must take."

"I don't want to hide myself in a cavern!" Anna cried. "I don't want to be feared as I fear her!"

"Never should a chosen one be feared! Never need you live as she did! I have wondered why she hid herself. It can only have been to keep us from knowing what she was doing. I can't believe . . . For you, live as you will. You must gain the wisdom that will fashion your own golden band. You are needed for that."

"My children need me! I will take the power I have and go at once!"

"No! You cannot leave a second time without the understanding that comes with the fashioning of your circle of knowledge. You would die in the Wood of Cris Thon, if not before."

Anna was stunned. "Eddris—she knew I would try to follow. And this?" She touched the side of her face. "My protection gone! Not even with this?" She held up the golden band. "Can't I take this with me and so live? The power in it . . ."

Stilthorn shook his head. ". . . is not for you."

"And so I can't help them? They're so young! They don't know! Eddris—her power! Where are they? There's no one to help them!"

"Don't weep, my Teyapherendana." Stilthorn took her wrists and gently drew her hands away from her face. "You are indeed beautiful! As your mother was. Come now. I would show you something."

He led her to a door and into a room filled with books and artifacts, the walls covered with drawings and paintings.

"The story of your man," Stilthorn said. "Here—how he learned to protect himself with stones, here those clubs and bows he used in the hunt. On this wall, his drawings to show his reverence for the creatures that sustained him. Here the instruments of his art, music, and dance. These are the tools he used, the plow and the hoe, the net for fishing. And here . . ." He took down a sharp bladed sword. ". . . his weapons. His means of killing his fellow men."

He returned the sword and chose another, a shorter blade, taking down scabbard and belt and fastening them around his waist.

"What sword is that?"

"It is the sword last used by Benelf—his son's, taken by

Benelf when his own was broken by Fel. Come. You've seen enough."

In his study he took up a shoulder strap and his cape. Then he held out his hand. "Now, give me the circlet. As I said, it will do you no good. But I . . . Give it to me! Yes. There. Now we will talk of other things for we will soon say good-bye."

"Why? What are you going to do? Why are you wearing Benelf's sword? He was slain when he carried that sword! What shall *I* do?"

"We will go to the great library of Ahln where all of our knowledge lies. You will find the volumes your mother wrote. Read them. Her wisdom will comfort you, bring you to understand what it is to be of the Nedoman." He held up his hand to stop her from speaking. "When you've finished your study, come to me. We will talk of what you've learned."

"But my children! Eddris—her golden band!"

He smiled.

"This?" The ring of gold gleamed in his palm. "She cannot use it while I hold it. I will keep it while I search for . . ." His smile widened as his fingers curled around the band. Softly, and with both wonder and delight in his voice he murmured, " . . . my grandchildren."

11

Why are you doing that?"

That girl! Watching him! Scroot glared at her. "Because I'm trying to guess which of the little dots will turn up. It's a game." His lips pulled tight over his teeth in a grimace. "Now go away."

She didn't go. She squatted beside him. "Don't you know?"

"No I don't." But I should, he grumbled to himself as he shook the cubes between his palms. He said he'd weighted them for me.

"There'll be three dots on one and six on the other," she said as he threw them down.

She was right.

"How did you know that?"

She didn't answer him.

"What will it be this time?"

"I can't tell until you shake them."

He shook them.

"One has one dot and one has four dots."

He threw them down. Right again. He stared at the dice.

"But it's not what I want." He scowled.

"What do you want?"

"I want five on one and two on the other. Or six on one and one on the other. Or three on one and four on the other."

"Why?"

"Because they all come to seven and seven is my lucky number. That's why."

"Why don't you make them do it?"

"I've been trying to!" And if I ever come across that cheating thief I'll twist his nose until he sneezes into the clouds! Curse that chit of a girl! Why does she look at me that way?

"Aren't you going to shake them again?"

He threw the dice. A two and a five.

"More like!" he muttered and threw them again. A one and a six. Again. A four and a three. "But I can't have it all three ways." He threw again. A one and a six. Five more times he threw, and five more times the dice added up to seven. He stared at the little girl.

"It's a silly game," she said and stood up. "I'm tired of it. I'm going to help Keld with the fish."

Scroot's hand trembled as he rubbed it across his mouth. If she *had* made the dice turn up seven . . . He'd have to find a way to force her. What might make her do it? He'd find a way. When he did, he'd find a way to keep her, and that soon. The gates of Adnor were not far down the road, and the sign of the Rusty Crow was just inside the gate, and he had a thirst beyond believing. There was hunger in the faces of those two for something beside fish, so they'd all sit down together. When it came to paying, there was the ring. Be rid of the boy and off to Wilp with the chit. No one to suffer. He got to his feet.

"Come on," he called. "I'll take you where you want to go."

"No, no, it's not the potter's house. It's a place for drinking . . . and eating," Scroot added hastily as Keld hesitated. "Come in, come in. They'll serve you all you can eat and more. Then we'll hunt for your potter." He herded them through the door, pushed his way to a table, and elbowed room on the bench for the three of them.

"Everything you have for my friends here!" He waved his hand at the wench laden with platters. "You!" He snapped his fingers at the boy with the tray of mugs. "Here! And I'll want it filled again." He buried his nose in the froth.

Elylden sat close to Keld. This was a stranger place than anything she had ever imagined. There was such a confusion that her head felt tight above her eyebrows. The room was dark with smoke, crowded, and noisy. The smell of it gagged her—rancid grease and unwashed bodies, old wool, wet dogs, and sour ale all mingled with that of a

lifetime of cooking, as well as that of the whole pig turning on a spit and dripping fat into the fire. A haunch of
beef just taken from a boiling pot was being cut into
chunks on the board. The cook's apron was smeared with
red and brown, and stiff with a thousand wipings of his
greasy hands.

She dropped her eyes to her own hands clenched
tightly in her lap. They should not have come here even if
they were hungry. They should have gone at once to the
street of the blind potter.

Just then there appeared before her and Keld a trencher
of meat and gravy and two slabs of bread. Elylden looked
sideways at Keld. He reached for the bread. Of course,
if you were very hungry . . . She would think herself
into old Pareth's cottage, with the smoke from the fire
and the light from the small window with the gray parchment covering it and the goat standing by. Yes, the goat!
It smelled much the same. She would shut away everything but the bread. The bread was heavy and hard to
chew, but soaked in a little gravy she could bring herself
to pretend she was in Pareth's cottage. Elylden licked her
fingers.

But old Pareth is dead!

She looked up quickly. Something was wrong! That
horrid man, Scroot, was standing up and searching through
the rags he wore, all the places pockets should be and
other places besides.

"A pickpocket here, I say. I had money with me. A

pouch in my shirt. Someone's taken it. Eh! Don't worry! The boy here will pay."

"I've no money!" Keld too was standing, facing a man twice the size of both himself and Scroot put together. "I told you so on the road."

"You've a ring. It's gold. See?" Scroot pointed to Keld's hand and turned to the man. "You'll have that for your bad meat and moldy bread! And for the flat ale too!"

"No! I can't give that," Keld said and doubled his fist. "It's my father's!"

"Belongs to your da, does it!" said the big man. "Well not anymore. Give it! Or would you rather take twenty lashes and spend your days rotting in a prison hole?" He seized Keld by the collar.

"Now, now, now!" Scroot cried. "Let's not be hasty. A throw of the dice and we'll call it even. Sevens, I say, three times in a row! A three and a four." His eyes slid toward Elylden. "Who'll take me? A three spot and a four and the meal is ours. Anything else and you take what the boy has and do with him what you want."

You must be aware, Elylden, alert to all things.

Elylden's eyes met those of Scroot. The man's eyelid drooped, and then he shifted his look to the side. The game, for Keld's ring!

"I'll chance you, but not with any of yours. You'll use mine." A gawky fellow with a squint leaned across the table. "Three times seven. If it's your luck, I pay for the meal."

"Done!" Scroot cried and scooped up the dice slapped on the board.

The big man tightened his hold on Keld, one arm around his throat, one grasping his wrist. The room quieted. People were watching.

"A three and a four!" Scroot repeated.

Elylden fixed her eyes upon his hand as he shook it sideways and then threw down the dotted cubes.

"A three and a four!" someone cried.

"A cheat!" shouted the squint-eyed one.

"They're your own!" Scroot cried, and then again, "Sevens! A one and a six!"

Again Elylden watched his hand.

"A one and a six!"

A last murmur in the room died as Scroot took up the dice a third time. "Sevens three times. A two and a five." All eyes were fixed on his hand.

For all the crowd, the room may as well have been empty. No one who understood. All thoughts were the same—all but . . . Elylden looked from one to the other of the faces of those standing around the table.

You must be aware!

No. Not that one. There! *That* one!

A slight, wiry, dark-eyed young man was the only one whose attention was not upon Scroot's hand but upon Elylden's face. Their eyes locked.

There was a cry. "A one and a two!"

"You lose! You lose it all!"

"You little witch!" Scroot's voice rose. He reached for Elylden, but she backed quickly against Keld.

"Throw him out!"

Two men seized Scroot and hustled him toward the door.

"Now, the ring, boy, and the law for you besides for helping a scoundrel. For the girl there, I've work for her in back!"

Keld began to struggle, but the man tightened an arm across his throat and with his other began twisting his wrist.

"You've had your fun!" A new voice cut in, and the sharp slap of a hand upon the board brought sudden attention to the dark-eyed young man. "Here's the price of the meal. Let him go!" Three coins lay on the table.

"Who's he to you?" asked the big man, who was not about to let go of Keld just yet.

"My sister's son—and daughter. Shana, isn't it? And Terach?" Elylden nodded. "I've not seen them for seven years, or I'd have known at least the boy. I thought they'd be alone, not with that weasel. The ring is his father's. They've come to serve the Lady Sirdde."

At the mention of that name, Keld was released quickly, and the big man scooped up the coins. "You'd better not show your faces here again," he muttered.

The young man hurried Keld and Elylden from the room.

"This way," he said, motioning Keld to be quiet, and

turned them into the street and then from one street to another, each more crowded than the last. At a corner Keld took his arm. "Wait. I want to thank you for helping us. But we're not who you think. We're . . ."

"Oh yes we are," Elylden broke in quickly. "You're Terach and I am Shana. Thank you, Uncle . . . ?"

The man looked down at her. Suddenly he threw back his head with a laugh. "Feirek. Your Uncle Feirek. You're a quick-witted lass!" He touched his hand to his forehead, then held it out.

Elylden took it gravely. She liked the feel of it. Bony and firm.

"And you?" He turned to Keld.

"I thank you—Uncle." He half-smiled as he took the offered hand. "Now will you tell us where we can find the street of the blind potter?"

The smile faded from their new acquaintance's face.

"Street of the blind . . . ?" He stared at Keld. Then he whistled. "Ah. Yes. Well. Let's see." He scratched his head. "Where . . . ? Maybe if we ask . . . if there's some-one . . . I'll see if I can find out."

He looked over his shoulder and all around. "Come along."

He turned abruptly and began walking in a new direction. Keld strode beside him. Elylden had to trot to keep up with them. She reached out to take Keld's hand. Evening was coming, and the narrow, twisting streets of Adnor were growing more and more shadowed.

★ ★ ★

Scroot picked himself up. Well, it was a start for the evening, but not enough to—whup! Why, they'd let them go! Luck! He'd follow that little witch! *There* was a package he wanted in his pocket!

arrow open markets lined the streets. Feirek pushed through a stall filled with clay pots and knocked at a door at the back.

"Is this the shop of the . . . ?" Keld began, but Feirek interrupted.

"It would be better if you didn't speak of the man or the place."

The door opened a crack. "What do you want?"

"I've brought you a duck and a goose. Open the door!"

Elylden wondered where he kept the birds. He carried no sack, and there was no room for two such large ones beneath his tunic.

"Feirek!" A woman's voice rose, and the door opened at once.

"Exactly right, dear Arela." He hurried Keld and Elylden into a room, half-lighted, small. He closed the door and lifted a wooden bar, dropping it into the iron brackets on either side of it.

"I've been hunting." He pushed his lank black hair back from his face and kissed the woman on the mouth.

Arela, a young woman with a kerchief around her head, laughed and pushed him away. "I can see that."

Again Elylden was puzzled. Feirek carried no bow. She eyed the woman, noticing first the white scar that curved down her forehead to cut across an eyebrow. But her dark eyes were lively and curious, and Elylden forgot the scar at once.

"I am sure you can. I'm afraid there are others who have seen it too, so we'll be careful. This is Terach and this is Shana. They'll spend the night. Is there a rug for them to lie on?"

"We can't stay here!" Keld protested. "We have to find . . ."

"Not tonight." Feirek again interrupted. "It's no walk for the night. The streets are full of robbers and cutthroats. We'll go in the morning. Now then, Arela?"

"There's a mat." Her quick smile showed crooked and slightly protruding teeth. "Have you had your supper? There's bread." She lighted a tallow lamp with a stick from the fireplace. "Did you bring cheese, Feirek?"

"They've had their supper," Feirek said. "They need sleep. We'll all sleep early. Why don't you fetch the mat?"

Elylden pursed her lips and glanced sideways at Keld. Her brother was looking around the room. Her eyes followed his. There were a table and three chairs. A small cupboard with tin plates and some mugs and pots in it stood against one wall. A few sticks burned on the hearth.

Arela vanished behind a curtain and returned with a rug and a shawl.

Elylden pulled off her shoes. She was glad to lie down, stretch, and then draw her knees up. "Keld?" she whispered.

"What?"

"This isn't a good place."

"This house?"

"No. Adnor. It's different from Wode Nen, but I don't like it any better. It's even worse."

"Maybe it'll be different at the potter's."

"Maybe." She was quiet for a while. She could hear a low murmur from the other room. Feirek and Arela were talking too.

"Keld?"

"What?"

"You should hide your ring."

"I already did. It's on the chain Anna gave me to wear."

"Where are we going to find money to pay for things?"

"We'll have to ask the potter."

"What if he doesn't tell us?"

"Anna said he would help us."

"Did you see the pot on the shelf here?"

"I saw some pots."

"There's one that's like one we have—had. One that

Anna made. That's partly why I think this house is all right. Do you like Feirek?"

"Yes."

"Do you like Arela?"

"Yes."

"I do too. Why do you think he barred the door?"

"Anna always barred the door."

"Yes, but that was because the people of Wode Nen didn't like us. Do you think the people of Adnor don't like Feirek and Arela?"

"You heard him say there were robbers."

"There's nothing here to rob but tin plates."

"He said there were cutthroats."

"What's that?"

"People who kill other people."

"You mean in a war? Like Benelf of the Hundreds and Fel?"

"No. Just because—because they want to."

"Why should they do that?"

"I don't know, Elyl. Go to sleep. You heard Feirek say the street of the blind potter was far away. Anna said Adnor was a village, but it's a much bigger one than Wode Nen. We may have a long walk tomorrow."

Keld closed his eyes. Their first sight of the town had made him uneasy. A squat stone fortress atop a hill with a great mass of houses clustered below, it was surrounded by a river and thick, high earthen walls. The streets they had come through were as airless, cramped, and crowded as the room in the Rusty Crow. He longed for the space and freedom of the mountain.

Elylden was quiet. So many people here! She had never known anything but the village of Wode Nen, and Anna seldom took Keld and her there because people looked at them strangely. Sometimes boys shouted at them, but they always ran away when Anna turned her face toward them.

Sometimes they went to old Pareth's. Sometimes he came to them and brought things for Anna. He had brought Elylden a toy sheep made with sticks jointed together and a bit of wool glued to its back. It was her friend. She kept it in her apron pocket and told it everything, because the cat would yawn, the pony would rather eat, and the chickens understood nothing.

She hadn't thought to bring the sheep with her. It had burned with the house. Tears filled Elylden's eyes. Wode Nen was a bad place, but Anna had explained about their fear. Adnor was worse. *People killed one another,* and there was no one to explain why, no one to look at them to drive them away. There was not even her sheep to talk to.

"Keld?"

But Keld was asleep.

"I won't tell anyone," she whispered to herself. "I'll hide it the way Keld hid his ring. I'll pretend it's on a chain around my neck under my dress the way Keld's ring is under his shirt. I'll pretend it's Anna's gift to me. Keld will always know, but I'll tell him not to tell anyone. I'll only use it for myself and Keld. I won't play any more games with it. Ever." The corners of her mouth pulled down. Everything was different. She hated it! They should go somewhere else!

Scroot settled himself in a doorway. Which door was it over there? He'd see them come out in the morning. Then . . .

A hand gripped his shoulder. A voice was in his ear. "There's someone would like to hear your story about those two. Come on now, and no fuss. There's always a gallows for a scoundrel."

13

erach? Shana? Wake up!" Feirek was shaking them. Keld sat up and squinted at the wavering light.

"Put on your shoes. We're going now."

"Is it morning already?"

"It's between midnight and dawn. That's morning, isn't it?"

Elylden sat up, yawned, and lay down again.

"Come on, Elyl." Keld shook her.

"This way." Feirek took them behind the curtain that divided the room. There he and Arela bent to lift and slide the cover from an opening in the floor. There was a ladder beneath it.

"Lead the way, Arela," Feirek said, handing her the lamp.

Arela nodded, took the lamp, and went backward down the steep, narrow steps. Elylden followed and then Keld. Arela held the lamp high so that Feirek could see to lift the boards and slide them tightly into place above their heads.

"Go on," Feirek murmured. "There's no room to pass."
They were in a stone passage so narrow there was
scarcely space to turn around. Elylden followed Arela.

"Where are we going?" Keld asked. "Why . . . ?"

"It's a way of coming to the street of the blind potter,"
Feirek said. "It's safer not to talk."

Aware of his quickly beating heart and dry mouth, Keld
asked himself, Is this being afraid? He had never been
afraid of a man until the host in the Rusty Crow had
seized and held him so that he could scarcely breathe.
Then he was both angry and panic-stricken. What kind of
people were these? He would have been glad to find
some way to earn the money to pay for the food. But not
his ring!

He slipped a finger beneath his collar to assure himself
that the chain was still there. He would ask the blind potter about his father's kin. If they found someone, good. If
not, they would leave this place and hunt for the Knights
of Ahln. He would take Elylden. Bothersome as she could
be, he could not leave her here—not even with the blind
potter.

The boy stumbled. He put his hand against the damp
stones of the wall to steady himself. They must have
already walked as far as they lived from Wode Nen, and
still they walked! He scowled. His mind was clearing of
the confusion he had felt when he first awakened. Was
the man really taking them to the blind potter? Why
through a hole in the floor? What kind of place . . . ?

There were no answers to these or a dozen other questions that came to him.

The passageway ended at last. Arela pushed open a door, and they came into a sour-smelling cellar full of great kegs. Another door took them up a flight of stairs. At a word from Feirek, Arela blew out the lamp. A faint light came from a window. Ten steps to a third door, and they were out on a cobbled street. The lopsided moon shone pale through fog. A black mass of houses rose on one side. On the other the river flowed, the dark water whispering against the earthen wall.

With a word of warning to move quietly, and keeping in the shadows, Arela and Feirek hurried Keld and Elylden along the street. They had not gone far when a low singing came to their ears. It rose quickly to a shriek, and suddenly two cats rolled from a doorway, a growling, screaming, hissing, spitting ball of fur and claws. Almost at once there was a low rumble followed by a deep bark, and a dog rushed from an alley. Keld had never imagined a dog so huge—almost as large as their pony! With a ferocious snarl, it hurled itself toward the cats.

The cats had instant and separate affairs of their own. Almost as quickly, Feirek pushed Arela, Keld, and Elylden into the recess of a doorway, but the dog had seen them. It turned toward them.

Pressed against her, Keld felt Arela shudder.

"No!" she whimpered.

On his other side, Elylden dropped to her knees. Feirek, tense, his arms spread, crouched in front of them facing the dog. The animal stood quietly, its head lowered, its tongue lolling from the side of its mouth.

There was the sound of running feet and men's voices. Reflected light flickered on the mist-dampened cobbles.

"Where is he?"

"Did he find someone?"

"No. There he is. There's no one. It was cats. Fool dog!"

A whistle pierced the night. The dog started toward the voices, then stopped to sniff at and mark a post.

"Get here!" a voice shouted, and the dog trotted from sight.

Elylden stood up.

By now Arela was trembling so violently that Feirek had to hold her. "He's gone," he whispered over and over. "He's gone, Arela. Don't ask me how or why. I didn't expect one to be here. They must be looking in more places. Don't cry. We're almost there."

Keld's own heart was beating quickly, though he didn't know what harm might have come to them. The dog had been no threat. Perhaps it was the men who frightened her. What were they looking for?

With shaking hands Arela covered her mouth to stifle her crying.

"Follow us," Feirek murmured to Keld and, his arm around her shoulder, drew Arela from the doorway.

"Sirdde—I hoped she would soften him, make him stop!" Arela's low voice was choked by a sob.

"Hush!" Feirek murmured. "Maybe she will in time. Hush!"

They paused in an alley while Feirek looked up and down a wider street. Keld saw that morning was near. Elylden's hand found his.

"Now!" Feirek murmured. "Run!"

But Elylden pulled at her brother's arm. "Keld, Keld! Wait! I smell the Wood of Cris Thon!"

Keld paused and lifted his head to sniff at the air so laden with the scent of the river.

"I don't," he said.

"It's gone now," she told him.

"Don't wait! Hurry!" Feirek warned. "The dog . . ."

Elylden's fingers tightened on Keld's.

"He'll be back, that dog," she whispered as they ran.

14

la was wakened by the hound, whining and scratching at the door.

"What is it this time, Zar?" She half-roused herself, addressing her husband's back as he bent to tie his bootlaces.

"I don't know! But it's the last time he stays in the house. He belongs in the shed with the mule so there he'll go."

By the gray light Ila knew that morning was coming. It was time to be up and about. She didn't want to be up and about.

"I've told you so often enough," she grumbled. "He kept us awake half the night. Quiet, Ragat!" she scolded.

Zar straightened his back and sighed. He was fond of the hound. Usually he was a well-behaved dog. He hoped the whining had nothing to do with the woman and the cart. He rose to his feet and went to the door, shoving the hound aside with his knee so that he might open it. His hand was on the latch when he heard the tapping.

Zar froze. Ragat sat back with such a look on his face as Zar had never seen on a hound—neither hostility nor cheerful anticipation. His ears flopped forward, his mouth pulled to an O, his eyes fixed on the door, the dog seemed as startled and expectant as Zar felt.

Again there came a rap.

Zar swallowed and opened the door. He gasped, and the hair on his arms and the back of his neck stood stiff.

The sun's first rays had just shot over the peaks and came into Zar's eyes, almost blinding him. It outlined the body of the dark figure that stood there and set the edges of him all aglow, a dazzling brilliance leaping from his shoulders and head.

"Good morning." The voice, deep and resonant, sent a vibration through Zar and made him feel as if he had been reduced to a quivering bowl of jellied mutton broth.

Zar staggered backward and raised his hand to shade his eyes.

"I hope I haven't disturbed you so early." The stranger glanced at the hound and slowly extended the back of his hand toward him.

Ragat stretched his neck, touched the hand with his wet nose, and looked into the man's face with such a question on his own that if Zar had been in any other state of mind, he would have laughed.

As it was, he shook his head feebly. "No, no. No bother. It's late for me—for us," he corrected, hearing the scrape of the bone rings as the curtain was drawn to hide the bed behind him.

"What do you . . . What can I . . . Where . . . That is, have you lost your way? Won't you come in?" He was not sure he wanted to be so hospitable, but could not seem to help himself. He again backed up.

"I thank you."

Stepping past the dog, the stranger entered. He was a tall man with dark eyes and dark hair. Clean-shaven, his features were as craggy and strong as the rocky peaks above. There was no telling his age. Zar closed the door against the sharp wind, and Ragat sank down as if his legs were as much turned to clabber as Zar's own.

"I . . . ah, we . . . Won't you sit down? I was about to build the fire. Mornings are cold on the mountain, midsummer or not."

He turned to the fireplace and was surprised to see that the embers from the night's fire still glowed. A stick or two and a small log soon produced a warm blaze. He lifted the kettle from the hob, thinking to fill it, but it was heavy enough and he set it over the flames on the trivet. In half a minute it was steaming.

Frantically Zar searched for some matter to talk of, but he had already mentioned the weather and could find nothing else in his mind.

The stranger did not offer a word, but appeared weary and content enough to rest. He had thrown back his heavy cloak to show a wide shoulder belt across his tunic and a belt at his waist as well. His shirt was of so fine a weave Zar could not see the thread of it, and the color changed as he moved, now red, now blue, now of deepest purple.

The corners of Zar's mouth twitched. He hadn't cried in more than twenty years—since his pa had beat him, in fact—but now, more than anything, he wanted to cry. It was foolish of course. There was no reason. He cleared his throat and swallowed. Then he saw the short scabbard and the hilt of a sword. His hands turned cold.

Ila came from behind the curtain.

"Law, Zar!" she exclaimed. "You've the fire made and the water hot so soon! We'll have porridge in no more than a minute. You're welcome to our house, poor as it is." She addressed the stranger. "You'll breakfast with us? There's bread and good cream . . ." The rush of words slowed, which was odd for Ila. ". . . from the cow. Zar, fetch some from the cellar and . . ."

Zar came to her aid.

"Th-this is Ila. My . . . my . . . my . . . my wife," he stammered. "A fine wife she is and makes a finer porridge."

The stranger looked up, a glint of humor in his dark eyes. "I'm sure she is finer than porridge," he said. "Thank you, I will accept your offer." His eyes went from one to the other and then turned to travel around the room. "This was your father's house?"

"Oh—ah yes! And my grandfather's and his father's before him. It's scarcely changed except for the blankets and the new curtains Ila brought when we married sixteen years ago. I . . . I suppose they're not so new anymore." Zar added the last in some surprise and confusion that what he had always considered new were now doubtless quite old.

Ila poured water from the kettle to the pot on the grate and stirred in the groats. She did this and that, seeming not able to find her tongue. Now she set a cup of tea before the stranger and, not looking full at him, which was not her way either, remarked nervously, "You're up the mountain early."

"Down the mountain," he corrected, nodded his thanks and put the cup to his lips.

At those words Zar felt as if he had been reamed out and left hollow from pate to sole. He sat down heavily and cupped his hands around the hot mug Ila set before him.

"Oh? Ahh!" Ila sat down herself and cradled her cup between her palms.

Frowning slightly, the stranger put down his cup, looked intently at it for a second, and then lifted it again to his lips. Setting it down a second time, he smiled. "An excellent tea, Ila."

"Oh, is it?" she gasped, and both she and Zar lifted their mugs too.

"It is!" Zar exclaimed, staring in surprise at the brew. "What have you done with it, Ila?"

"I don't know!" she cried. "It tastes of flowers. It doesn't need a bit of honey!"

"None at all," the stranger agreed.

"My!" Ila said and sipped with pleasure.

The porridge too was excellent and the cream came from the pitcher in thick clots, richer than Zar had ever seen or even dreamed of.

The meal was continued in silence, Zar shaking his head now and again. Never had groats tasted so sweet. Never had Ila's bread—though always good—set his mouth to watering so.

When they had finished, the stranger rose to his feet.

"I thank you," he said simply. "Now I must be on my way."

Zar rose quickly, pushing back his chair with a loud scraping.

"I . . . I, ah, will see you to the door." He leaped ahead to open it. The stranger drew his cloak around him and followed the man into the sun's light. "Do you know your way?" Zar asked.

The stranger nodded, then said, "The winter sun will keep the cold from your dwelling, Zar. The summer storms will bring no flood to your doorstep. Good-bye." He touched Zar's shoulder, then held out his hand.

"Good-bye," Zar murmured. He took the offered hand with some fear, but found nothing but strength and warmth in it.

He watched as the man rounded the boulder that sheltered the house, then, half-tripping over the dog, ran after him to see him stride down the mountain. Ragat leaned against Zar's leg and watched with him.

The stranger never once looked back.

When Zar returned to the cottage, Ila asked, "Where did he go?"

"Down the mountain."

"Round about?"

"No. Straight toward the Wood of Cris Thon."

"What was his name? You didn't think to tell me!"

"I didn't think to ask."

There was no one in the pothouse of Wode Nen who did not wonder who he was, but the innkeeper only asked, "You . . . seek someone here?"

"I seek the dwelling of Ericoth of Eneth," said the tall, dark man. "I seek also his daughter and the son of his wife Anna by her first husband."

There was such a silence in the room that the sound of a moth's wings fluttering about an oil lamp could be heard. A young man, his drink lifted halfway to his lips, clapped the mug to the table and rose to his feet.

"You're too late," he said bitterly. "They're dead. All of them. Anna, the boy, the girl . . ." He looked around angrily. "Don't ask me how or why. Ask them!" He waved his arm in a half-circle, took up his jacket, and stamped from the inn, slamming the door behind him.

"Dead?" The stranger's eyes went from one face to another.

One man cleared his throat. "There was a fire."

"They lived by themselves—up from the village," a second put in.

"Burned to the ground before anyone knew," said a third.

The stranger rose. "Will you show me the place?"

For a moment no one moved, then half a dozen rose.

The innkeeper himself wiped his hands on his apron and came forward. The group of men, keeping close together, led the way to the end of the village and continued on a path up the mountain. The stranger came behind them. No word was spoken.

When they came to the meadow, the men stood aside, and the stranger walked to the edge of the pile of rubble that still reeked of smoke. With the toe of his boot he touched a heavy green log that lay before the charred door posts.

"What a pity," he said. "Wode Nen would have been honored."

Though the evening twilight did not let them see his eyes, each felt the dark look go through him. The innkeeper cleared his throat.

"Would you want a room for the night?" he asked.

"I'll not stay here," the stranger said.

The men felt themselves dismissed. As they returned on the path through the groves of hazel, only the innkeeper looked back. He stumbled and almost fell, then ran to catch up with the others. He did not see the stranger go swiftly through the still-hot ashes to the only thing left standing—the stone chimney and oven at its side.

The man opened the iron door of the brick oven, drew four objects from it, and ranged them on top of it. For some time he gazed upon these, studied them, taking up each in turn and looking at it closely, passing his hand over and around the features and setting it down again.

"Forgive me for not telling you, my Teyapherendana, but Eddris lied when she told you only a shred of your power remained to you. She could not take any of it from you. If you gave all that you had to your daughter, she possesses all that is possible for a child born this side of the Crags of Ahln. It is indeed great. As for your son . . ."

He took up one of the busts and once more let his fingers caress the features. "Your gift will make it difficult for him, especially if what you say of man is true, as I begin to think it is." He frowned, turning the bust in his hand. "Compassion asks more strength and courage than killing has ever done!

"Again, forgive me, my daughter. The work of your hands is of beauty beyond thinking, but Eddris must not learn so soon the faces of your children, nor those of their fathers." A bust now in each hand, he looked closely at them, murmuring. "She has been here but has not seen you. She does not know you as I do. Now she searches beyond. Still, I cannot leave it to chance that she will not return."

He hesitated a moment. Might she use her power to find them quickly? That heinous a means? So monstrous a risk! The destruction of . . . If she did, she would be waiting for them. What image would she use? He shook his head. Then, with great deliberation, he hurled one fired bust against the smoke-blackened stone of the chimney, then the other. The remaining two followed. All were shattered.

He scooped up a handful of their dust and, straightening, waved his other hand in a circle. A ring of blue flame rose from the ruins, and he scattered the bits of baked clay into it.

"Courage to courage, grandson of Benelf," he murmured, "and fire to fire, daughter of Ericoth, children of Anna."

He continued to scatter the broken pieces of the clay figures into the flames until not one bit of powder or breath of their dust remained.

The fire died away, and Stilthorn took the path that went through the meadow toward the spring and on to the falls of Gresheen.

15

eirek hurried them across the street and herded them into another alley. Again he led them through a maze of wynds so narrow that the over-hanging houses almost touched. The stench of the gutters was anything but the sharp, wild scent of the Wood of Cris Thon.

At the bottom of a flight of stairs he tapped at a door. It was opened and shut quickly behind them.

A short passage brought them to a long, low, heavily-beamed room. Sleepers lay on mats scattered on the stone floor. At the end of the room, before a fireplace, four men and two women watched a game of chess being played. They turned to greet Feirek and Arela and to stare at Keld and Elylden. A white-haired man, one of the players, rose.

"What's this?" he asked.

"You mean 'who,' " Elylden said before Feirek could say a word.

The man looked down at her in surprise, then smiled.

"You're half right. I should have said 'What is the meaning of this and who are these young people.' But you see we have come to cut short our words."

"If you're too short you say the wrong thing," she told him.

"Elylden!" Keld warned, recalling the crowd in the Rusty Crow and the tightness of the arm across his throat.

"Shana." She corrected him quickly. Keld bit his lip.

"It's all right." The man held up his hand. "She deserves an explanation. We cut short our words because if we're too long-winded, our breath may end on the gallows."

"Then it's better not to say anything." Elylden's eyes were fixed on his face. Keld knew the pout of her lips came when she was as thoughtful and serious as ever she could be. All the same, he wished she would not speak so to a stranger in Adnor.

But again the man smiled. "Perhaps you're right."

"I am," she said, closed her mouth, and began looking carefully at everyone in the room, including those who slept.

"El—Shana is used to saying what comes to her mind. It saves wondering what she's thinking," Keld explained.

"May the powers that be protect her!" murmured the man who had opened the door.

Elylden's eyes came to his. "They do," she said.

"Wha—!" Such a look of surprise crossed his face that there was a burst of laughter from others who had been watching and listening.

"Come sit by the fire, all of you," another invited.

"Feirek, tell us who they are and where you found them and why you brought them here."

This Feirek did in a few sentences, ending with, ". . . and then Terach asked me to take them to the street of the blind potter."

Several of the sleepers had wakened and come to join those by the fire. With his last words faces that had shown interest, and no little irritation at the events in the Rusty Crow, were suddenly intent.

Staris, the white-haired man, cleared his throat. "Where do you come from, Terach, and who told you to ask for such a street?"

When Keld hesitated, eyes turned to Elylden, but though her steady look met theirs, she said nothing.

Keld began, "Perhaps you've not heard of the place. We come from near Wode Nen."

He went on to tell briefly and cautiously that their mother had sent them, of their walking for four days, their meeting with Scroot, and their coming to the alehouse. "Feirek has told you the rest."

"But what of the street? Who told you of that?" Staris asked.

"Our mother. She knew the potter when she was young. He taught her to shape clay. She said he would teach me, that he would help us."

He looked around the circle of listeners. Some seemed puzzled, others doubtful of his words. One man shook his head. What more was there to tell them? Keld chewed his lip. "She gave me three things to do. Learn to shape clay, look after El—my sister, and find my kin. There's a fourth I would do for myself," he added hesitantly.

"What is that?" Staris asked when the boy said no more.

Keld frowned. If he had told them this much, he may as well tell them all of it. "We followed the Knights of Ahln to the falls of Gresheen. I . . . I would find them and join them. Have you seen them?"

His question was answered only by even more startled expressions. The man who had shaken his head touched a finger to his temple.

"Oh, come now!" another exclaimed.

Feirek spoke sharply. "What of your father's ring, Terach. Have you lost it?"

Keld looked around the circle of faces, his eyes resting last of all upon Elylden, who sat close to him. Finally, with a slight frown, he ran his finger beneath his collar, drew out the chain, and unfastened it. He slipped the ring from the chain to his finger and held out his hand, curled to a fist, to show it.

"Ahhh!" exclaimed Arela and the two other women. A man whistled.

"You say your father gave you this ring?" Staris asked.

"It was his. He's dead. Anna gave it to me."

"Anna?" The word exploded from Staris' mouth.

"My mother."

A young man suddenly leaped to his feet. "It's madness!" he cried. "I don't believe any of it! Some traitor has given us away! They've been sent to find us!"

Others murmured and looked uncomfortable.

Keld was appalled. What had he said but the truth, and as simply and clearly as he could?

Elylden frowned. It was hard to sort out so many at once. Why had they asked all those questions just to say the answers were lies?

"Wait! Wait!" Staris cried as the talk grew louder. "Don't judge so quickly!" He too touched a finger to his temple and shook his head. As the talk quieted he turned to Keld. "Now then," he said in so kindly a way that Elylden thought perhaps she didn't like this man after all. "Tell us about your life near Wode Nen, about your mother, Anna, and about . . . the Knights of Ahln."

But Keld was put off by their doubts. "There's not much to tell."

Feirek leaned forward. "We want to know."

A woman also spoke with great earnestness. "We *have* to know!"

Keld would have been brief, but with each short sentence about the village, the little farm, Anna, the towering Crags of Ahln, there seemed to be a hundred questions that brought more and more explanation from him, even to the happenings of the night before they left the farm and the burning of the cottage. Elylden leaned against him, her eyes going from face to face of the listeners.

"And as well as telling you these histories, did she sing the ballads to you?" Toseny, the young man who had first leaped to his feet to deny Keld's words, leaned forward in excitement.

"I don't know what you mean—the ballads," Keld said. "She sang to us. Songs of times before. Of the Ancient Ones, the Giants, the Wizards. Songs of the great heroes. Some she told. Stories of the battles, of the last war between Benelf of the Hundreds and Fel. The march of the Wizards, the Women of the Nedoman, and the Knights of Ahln up the mountain from the Valley of Hune . . ." He hunched his shoulders, hearing for a moment the tone of Anna's voice describing it as if she had seen it herself. Suddenly he longed for her to be with them, to bring something to Elylden.

"Did you learn any of those ballads? Do you remember some of them?" Toseny persisted. He seemed almost to be holding his breath.

"Of course I do!" Keld exclaimed. "And so does Elylden."

"Elylden?"

"Shana!" He could not remember to call her by that strange name!

"Which is it?" Staris asked quietly.

Elylden stood up. "It's Elylden," she said and backed away. "And my brother is Keld. It was Feirek who told us what our names were here. But it's wrong to take a name that's not your own unless you're a deceiver. Anna has told us about deceivers. We're not that.

"Of course we remember the songs," she went on. She started across the room. She had reached the passageway when, raising her voice, she turned to add, "We know all of the ones she sang to us. And we know the rune of regis arcanum." She disappeared around the corner. For a moment no one moved. Then came the sound of the door opening, and both Arela and Feirek leaped to follow her. Before they came to the hall, she returned. With her was the huge dog they had seen in the street.

Arela stepped back with a cry. Others leaped to their feet. Feirek ran to the hall only to come back in half a minute. "There's no one there. She locked the door."

"Of course I did," Elylden said. "They were whistling for him on the street above, but too far on. Now they'll never find him." The girl and the dog crossed the room to the fireplace. The dog flopped down and stretched out, his long tail beating a lazy thump against the floor. As silent as stone, the group in the room watched as Elylden sat cross-legged beside him. Her hand caressed his head and fondled his ears.

"He's my friend," she said.

hey were taken up narrow stairs to a small room to sleep once more, Keld, Elylden, and the dog— Thosstoe she called him.

Elylden woke, disturbed by a dream. She leaned toward her brother.

"Keld? Keld! Someone knows! They're looking!"

But Keld did not waken. Her dream . . . She lay awake for some time, then whispered defiantly, "Anna didn't tell me not to!"

Once more she sat up. "Keld! Keld?"

She stretched a hand toward her brother. Soon she slept again, her fingers caught in the cord she had asked for and fastened around the dog's neck.

A pale sun shone through the window. The square of light on the floor was faint. On the mountain the sun was always bright, light and shadows crisp and clear. This fuzzy sunlight, this dim room, these forever questions—he and Elylden must find the potter. He tried to get her attention, but she was so engrossed with the dog he could get no clear sign from her.

"You see, it's difficult for us to believe you," Staris was saying, "because it was such a long time ago that Anna, the daughter of a shepherd . . ." he paused. "Was your mother beautiful?"

"She was . . ." Keld hesitated. "Yes. Except there had been a fire and she was scarred. But only on one side of her face."

"Yours is a different Anna because *our* Anna isn't the daughter of a shepherd," Elylden said suddenly. "Her father's name was Stilthorn."

Toseny snorted. Staris groaned and clapped his hand to his forehead. "Where have you heard these things? No! Don't tell me. Anna told you."

"Of course she did." Elylden had begged a comb of one of the women and was dragging it down the dog's spine. His back twitched and now and again a leg scratched in sympathy with a ticklish spot.

"It can't have been *that* long ago," Keld protested, "because she came to Wode Nen after she learned from the potter. My father came soon after. I was born less than a year after that."

"A year is a long time," Elylden said. "But Anna isn't as old as you are," she addressed Staris. "She has no white hair. She braids it and wraps it around her head in the daytime. She takes it down at night to comb. It's long like mine and if she isn't careful, she sits on it. Only mine is black like my father's, and hers shines like the ring she wears, especially in the firelight. Doesn't it, Keld?"

She finished combing Thosstoe, untied and retied the cord around his neck to leave a short leash.

Keld nodded, half a smile on his face. "Copper and gold, and curls and waves like flames."

Toseny, who sat at the table and scratched away on a parchment, stopped his writing, threw down the quill, and turned around. "My fingers are cramping. My imagination ran so wild all night I have kinks in my brain. The blind potter, Anna . . . These two come claiming . . . No! I'll write no more. I'll go to the great fane and ask Monancien himself . . ."

"Hush!" Staris held up a warning finger.

"Well, I would. Nothing is left to us here! *They* have the only histories! The ancient libraries would tell . . . I'd risk the guards to take these parchments!" He massaged his hand and fingers.

"Be careful of these writings," Staris said. "Hide them. Bury the truth—if truth it is—but live the lies," he added dryly.

"We're used to that! We don't even notice it anymore." Toseny rose and paced back and forth in the little room.

"No thought of our own can be spoken aloud. No learning, no expression of poetry, or dance, or art, or music! All but one of the libraries of the fanes have been destroyed. Whatever else is left is in the minds of the poets, like Feirek. We come here in secret to hear them, because they daren't speak aloud! If they do, they're slain!

"Blygen and his brutes . . . We have to mouth their beliefs, pretend to accept their sameness as our own! The pap of lies they choose to feed us is chanted in our ears. No other idea can be brought . . ."

"Hush! Enough!" Staris rubbed his forehead.

"No! Not enough! I burn to know! I burn to have the ideas of others laid before me so that I may examine them! To know what happened in other years—from the beginning of time!" His eyes flashed.

"But is this allowed me? No! Yesterday Sashen was hanged. And for what? Who knows? He probably forgot to button his coat again and was denounced as joining a plot against the life of Blygen. No shred of evidence! Yet he is the fourth one of us in a week! The fourth! Ever since that woman Blygen married came here!

"Sirdde! Three days from when he saw her, he took her to his bed and the searches, the murders have doubled! His wife—she's worse than he is! Today I heard she's hunting for children. What could she wring from them?" Toseny suddenly stopped pacing to point at Keld and Elylden. "Finding a place to hide the writings will be hard enough, but where are we to hide *them*?"

Elylden lifted her face. "We can hide ourselves, Keld and I."

"Oh can you? What do you know of this place? Who'll help you, eh? Do you have friends in the court of Blygen?" Toseny seized Elylden and pulled her to her feet. Keld leaped up. The dog rose, a rumble coming from his throat.

"Toseny!" Staris cried.

Of them all, Elylden was the least bothered. "I don't know what Blygen is, but I don't like it. It has a bad sound. We won't go there. We want to go to the blind potter. Why don't you take us to him?"

Staris sighed. "Because, Elylden, the blind potter has been dead for two hundred years."

Suddenly Keld could not breathe.

Toseny dropped Elylden's wrists and turned away.

"Doubtless your mother was telling you a story," Staris went on quietly. "She couldn't have lived so long ago. Somewhere she heard of Anna and the blind potter and told you of it as if it were herself."

"But she knew him! He taught her . . . She knew how to . . . She would never lie!" Keld tried to collect his thoughts. "At least you could take us to the street where he lived! There must be something there!"

Staris shook his head. "I didn't say she meant to lie. Some people imagine." He shrugged. "Besides, who knows what street it was? There have been fires, wars, invasion—the town has grown, been rebuilt and built again. What was it two hundred years ago? A small village? We don't know."

"But Feirek promised to take us! You mean he lied to us?"

Elylden moved close to Keld. Thosstoe followed her,

his nails clicking on the floor. He sat down on her foot, rested his head on her shoulder, and leaned so hard on her side that she was pushed against her brother. The girl fixed her dark eyes first on Staris, then on Toseny.

"They do know, but they don't want to tell us," she said into the silence that followed Keld's words. "They don't know much of anything else."

Toseny cleared his throat, dropped his eyes to the table and began shuffling the parchments he had worked at so long.

"You're wrong to think Anna would lie to us," Keld persisted. "Maybe the days on the mountain are longer than those in Adnor. Maybe twenty years there is two hundred years here."

"Time is time. The sun rises and sets. Twelve hours of day and twelve hours of night."

"No," Elylden said. "Time changes. Days are long and short and so are nights. In the winter night is almost all of it. In the summer on the mountain day swallows the night."

She paused, then said softly. "In the Valley of Hune the Midsummer Day is forever."

There was another short silence and then, "No, no, midsummer doesn't last," Toseny said irritably. "The days shorten soon enough. The nights . . . Why am I arguing with this child?" In exasperation he stamped to the window and peered through it into the street.

Elylden did not reply. But Keld knew that Toseny, like himself, had felt that peculiar turning of stomach at Elylden's words. When they were alone he must tell her that she should not say things the way she did, whatever that way was. People here didn't . . . Nothing was right! Anna, didn't she know? What was he to think? What were they to do?

Elylden was speaking again. "The pots she made were more beautiful than the one on Arela's shelf. Even with one hand that couldn't use the fingers she did better. She made other things too. People. One of me and one of Keld. And of our fathers. She knew how because the potter taught her. She knew everything!

"Tell them," she went on, turning to Keld. "Tell them the histories, if they want to know! Tell them of the old ones, the way Anna told us. Tell them in her way of how they were and are and always will be. Tell them of the giants and the wizards and of Benelf and how . . ." She stopped suddenly and looked from Toseny to Staris.

"If *you* know so much about it—that the blind potter died two hundred years ago, what happened to *your* Anna?"

Toseny turned from the window, and he and Staris looked at each other for a long moment before Staris answered her.

"No one knows."

"Well *I* know," Elylden said flatly. "She went to Wode Nen two years after she came here. It was before the potter died because she didn't know he died or she never would have sent us to this awful place."

She paused, then turned to Keld. "But there's one

thing. She told us how your father came, but how did *she* come to Wode Nen from here?"

Keld had suddenly been wondering the same thing. "Not by way of the falls. She could never have climbed the rocks. She would have come up though the Valley of Hune. As the Wizards did. As my father did." He touched his tongue to his upper lip. His mouth was dry.

"Tell them," Elylden whispered. "Say it, Keld!"

Keld closed his eyes and took a deep breath.

> *In the Valley of Hune,*
> *The timeless Valley,*
> *The sun and the moon and the stars are one.*
> *All golden in the day, all silver in the night,*
> *They stand still in their paths in the sky*
> *So no man grows old.*
> *In the Valley of Hune*
> *Dwell the Women of the Nedoman*
> *Whose knowledge and whose beauty*
> *Stay the sun and stars in their paths in the sky*
> *So that time stands still,*
> *So that They and the Knights and the Wizards*
> *Never grow old.*

Keld kept his eyes closed still a moment, hearing the echo of Anna's voice in his ear, seeing in his mind the look on her face, feeling the touch of her fingers on his cheek. The Women of the Nedoman! Anna? She had gone up the mountain to the Crags! And his father . . .

who had he been? When had he gone to the Valley of Hune? Why had he died?

Two hundred years! What kin of his would he find here? There might be none that anyone knew of! Even with the ring! They were alone, he and Elylden.

He was brought back to this place by Elylden's whisper.

"Just so. Keld says it the way Anna does."

The whisper roused Toseny. He snapped shut his mouth.

"You must tell me again," he said eagerly, seating himself with a scrape of the stool, and snatching up his quill. "Tell me again. Oh, quickly! That is, slowly enough for my writing! How did it begin?"

Just then shouts came from the street below, then silence, then a single voice proclaiming, "Ten gold pieces for the deliverance of the fair-haired boy who wears a gold ring with a black stone set in it. The ring was stolen from Blygen. A gift to him from his wife, the Lady Sirdde. The boy was her servant. Blygen will see justice done!"

In an instant Staris was beside Keld. He seized a handful of the boy's hair and pulled his head back to glare into his startled eyes.

"So that's where you got it—the ring! You serve the wife of Blygen!"

17

irdde!" Toseny hissed. "What torture did she use to get the words from one of us? The blind potter! A clever way to find us out! How long have you served her?"

"I don't know anything about her!" Keld cried trying to fight his way from the man whose other arm now encircled his chest. "I never heard of her or Blygen! Or *you* until last night!"

"You have now, and worse luck for us!" Staris said between his teeth. "Give that ring to me! We'll be rid of it—throw it in the gutter for anyone to find! And *you* . . ."

Toseny seized Keld's wrists, but there was no ring on his finger.

"It's on the chain around his neck!"

The door opened. "What are you doing? Are you mad? Leave him alone!" Feirek rushed into the room and pulled Toseny away from Keld. Grumbling, Staris too let go his hold. Crouching, Keld backed against the wall. Elylden, her arm over Thosstoe's back, skirted the room to stand beside her brother.

"Blygen's ring!" Staris said, glaring at the curled-back lips of the huge dog. "The boy was sent to find us, put us all on the gallows!"

"I brought the boy," Feirek said angrily. "The ring is nothing to Blygen. His wife wants it! Where did she hear of it? Let me see it!"

Still crouching, glaring at Feirek, Keld put his hand to his throat.

"You needn't give it to me," Feirek reassured him. "I just want to look at it—to be certain it's what I think it might be."

Keld was unwilling. He straightened and put his arm around Elylden.

"We want nothing to do with any of you," he said stiffly. "Let us go. We'll find our own way."

"Yes. To the gallows," Feirek said. "Or no, rather just two more bodies in the street. No name to them. Beggars from the country. Carried off in a cart to be dumped in a ditch called a common grave."

Keld flushed hot and then grew cold.

"Show me the ring," Feirek demanded, then his mouth twitched, pulling up on one side, his eyes fixed upon Keld's. "You must know there's more than one man in the world who has proven his identity with a bauble of some sort.

This I give you,
my son,
to always know your kin.
For in whatever place,
whatever time, whatever life . . .
whatever death by nature
or by infamy,
by war that's lost or won,
by this ring and by this stone
you will be known for yourself,
Son of Benelf.

Keld started. He'd known the verse forever! It had nothing to do with him! It was just by chance that his father's ring, like Benelf's, might help him find his kin.

If Keld was startled, Toseny was dumbfounded. "Where did you hear that?" he demanded of Feirek.

"It's Anna's, only *we* didn't tell it to him!" Elylden's underlip pushed out.

"I've known it all my life," Feirek said. "That's to say, I learned it from my father, and he from my grandfather. The libraries have been burned, but fire doesn't burn all knowledge."

"Maybe not for the poets," Toseny grumbled. "But for those of us with poor memories . . ."

"Those of you with poor memories learn to read and write," Feirek snapped. "Now, Keld!"

At least Feirek understood the importance of the ring.

Keld slipped his hand beneath his collar and drew out the chain. He ran his finger around the front of it, then put both hands to the back of his neck and drew them to the front. He felt his face grow numb.

"It's gone," he whispered.

They searched the floor, shook the rug.

"It couldn't have fallen!" Keld insisted. "The chain was fastened."

"Then someone took it! Who was in here while they slept?" Feirek's face was grim.

"Anyone could have been. The door wasn't locked. Any one of us . . ."

There was an awkward moment of silence. It was broken by a clattering on the stairs and Arela's frantic voice.

"Staris! Feirek! Quick! They're searching every house in the street! They're almost at our door!"

"Out, then! Feirek, you take them. No, not that way!" Staris had gone swiftly to the window to glance into the street. "There—the closet. Arela, go with them. Here, the parchments! Toseny, you fool to write so much!"

Staris snatched up the parchments, thrust them into Arela's hands, and pulled open a door to a small, cramped space filled with cloaks, sacks, and boots.

"We can hardly . . ." Feirek began, but Staris pushed aside the clothes and leaned against a board to force it aside.

"Quick!"

They crowded through, Feirek pushing Keld ahead of him.

"My ring!" the boy cried.

"Your life!" Feirek snapped.

"Not the dog!" Staris exclaimed.

"Yes, Thosstoe!" Elylden insisted, taking the dog by the rope and pulling him through after her. There was no time for argument.

They glimpsed a steeply descending stairway, and then the panel was closed behind them and they were left in darkness. There were muffled voices, the sound of scuffling, a cry, then silence. They waited, listening, scarcely breathing. They heard nothing more.

"We have to find our way out of here," Feirek murmured at last. "But there's no light. We'll break our necks."

Keld felt a touch on his sleeve, and Elylden's hand found his.

"Thosstoe will take us down the stairs," she whispered.

"He's a dog, not a cat to see in the dark," Feirek muttered.

"He has a light to show him." Elylden tugged at Keld's hand.

"What do you mean?" Feirek questioned.

"If she says so, it's so! Feirek? Arela? Hold to me."

They began an awkward descent in a darkness so thick Keld thought he must be dreaming, his eyes closed and a pillow over them. His fingers locked into his sister's, he steadied himself with his other hand against a rough wall. Feirek's firm grip was on his shoulder.

"Now we'll go this way."

There was no question this time. Elylden led them over rough ground. After a time Keld saw a band of light broken by dark vertical shadows. Soon they were among stout pilings that supported the floors of buildings above. The pale light came from the river's surface.

"Wait here," Feirek murmured and went to the water's edge. On returning he told them, "I know where we are. I'll find a boat when it's dark—a while yet. We'll keep back out of sight." He sat down, his back against a pile. Arela seated herself beside him.

Keld and Elylden too settled themselves. Elylden stroked Thosstoe. Keld, his arms on his knees, put his head down. His stomach knotted. He had failed Anna. He had lost the ring. Why hadn't he wakened when someone took it? He would never know who he was!

And would he ever find the Knights of Ahln? Probably not!

What else was there to lose? Once again his stomach knotted.

Elylden!

18

"lyl, wake up! Feirek has a boat!"

Elylden sat up and rubbed her eyes. Then she put out her hand. The dog was there. She rubbed his head and felt for the rope.

"You can't take the dog." Feirek's voice was firm.

"I have to."

"There are four of us—one too many as it is, except that you're small. The dog will sink the boat."

"I won't go without him."

"You'll come with us." Keld's voice had a tone she had never heard.

"You sound just like Anna," she grumbled.

"There's no time to argue. Let the dog go," Feirek said. "We'll stay close to the docks and banks. He can follow along if he wants."

"He'll want to," Elylden said. She bent to touch the dog's head with her own and murmured, "Don't let them find you."

"Who?" Arela asked.

"Anybody."

The dog followed them to the river's edge, and though he whined, he made no attempt to get into the boat. The craft, a shell of tarred hides stretched over a frame of bent wood, sank low, the water lapping the rim of it when Feirek, last of all, carefully stepped in.

The animal whined again as the man pushed away from the mooring and began guiding the tiny craft down the river. The quarter moon was high. By its faint light Keld could see the huge dog, a moving shadow among the posts, walking, trotting, then loping along the bank. On the other side of the river rose an earthen wall. From time to time a cloud passed over the moon, casting town and river into darkness.

Feirek paddled cautiously, using the oar to keep them in the shadow of the buildings, slipping between docks, and among moored boats, pushing them back into the current when they brushed against an abutment. There was only the lapping of water, the creaking of ropes, and the occasional splash as Feirek's oar dipped into the dark flow.

If he still followed them Keld could no longer see the dog.

A bridge loomed ahead of them. Feirek moved even more cautiously, holding the boat close to the shore. As they drifted beneath the bridge, there was the sudden baying of a dog, a shout, and a terrifying scream just above them.

Arela, sitting next to Keld, grew rigid. Feirek was close

enough to reach out and seize an iron ring set in the stone of the pier. He held the boat beneath the bridge against the current.

They waited. It was still now. Then from far off a different sound came to their ears. Again it was a dog, but this time a distant howling. The next moment an eerie moaning rose. It was the howling of many dogs, first from far away, then taken up by others, drawing nearer and nearer. It was not the baying of the hunt, or the snarl of attack, but the anguish of dogs suffering pain.

The doleful clamor grew, came closer until it rose just behind them. In the next instant they were struck by a force so strong Keld was thrown across Elylden. A sharp pain stabbed through his ears. The shell was driven forward. Feirek let go of the iron ring to keep from being pulled from the boat. They swirled around, coming from beneath the bridge to be caught in an eddy at the corner of the pier and tossed against the wall. For half a minute Keld clung to both Elylden and the edge of the boat. He was dizzy, his ears humming. Suddenly, the boat tilted violently, dipped, and overturned.

He swallowed only a single mouthful of water before his head was above the surface and he was drawing Elylden up beside him. They were still beside the bridge, caught in the slowly spiraling current at the corner of the pier, Feirek beside them. Arela's head bobbed up a second later. Feirek pulled her to him. The overturned boat slipped away into the river's onward flow.

There was a fifth head in the water. That of a dog.

The animal was paddling toward the stone wall. He clawed his way onto a sill that ran along the river's edge, stopped an instant to shake, and then proceeded up a steep stair beside the bridge. The four in the water swam to the stair and followed the dog.

Halfway to the top, Feirek, a finger to his lips, stopped to listen. Keld's ears were no longer ringing. The howling had stopped. There was only the muted rippling of the river.

Feirek sank down on the step. "What was *that*?" he whispered.

Neither Keld nor Arela answered. Elylden looked down the river. Keld sensed the tension in her arm that touched his, the scowl on her face.

"That," she said, "was . . ." Suddenly her whole body relaxed and she leaned against him. "Thosstoe."

"Not the dog! The other! Like a wall of wind but I swear no breath of air touched us! Whatever, we were still afloat! That dog deserves a beating! We would have been out of the town in half an hour!"

"No. They would have caught us," Elylden said.

"Who?"

"I don't know. You do. There are boats on both sides of the river there." She pointed downstream. "With people in them."

Feirek's head turned in the direction she pointed. "How do you . . ." he began, then muttered, "It wouldn't be the first time. It's the way they steal a living from people who fish at night." He waited a while longer, watching the river and listening. At last he put his mouth close to Arela's ear. She nodded. With a sign to keep silent, Feirek motioned Keld and Elylden to follow.

At the top of the wall they found Thosstoe waiting for them, his tongue, as usual, lolling from his mouth, his tail wagging slowly. Elylden knelt on the cobbles and put her arms around his neck.

"We haven't time to waste." Feirek scanned the dark street.

"I'm not wasting time," Elylden said, and got to her feet.

They set out, again slipping through alleys. Keld hated these narrow, littered wynds where the stench of rot and poverty gagged him.

The sky was growing light when they stopped before the door of a small shop in a street of decaying houses and open stalls.

"This is what you've been looking for," Feirek murmured and rapped. Then knocked again. Suddenly he pounded on the door with his fist.

"Open the door before we break it down!" he shouted hoarsely.

Keld was startled. Feirek would waken the whole street!

He continued to shout and beat on the door until, "What d'ye want?" came the quavering voice of an old man.

"Open the door or we'll break it down!" Feirek cried again.

"No! I've done nothing! I have nothing!" came the shaky reply.

"Open in the name of Blygen!"

There was a clanking and scraping and the sound of a key turning. The door opened a crack to show gray whiskers and frightened eyes.

"I've done nothing!" The stubbled chin shook.

"This is the shop of the blind potter," Feirek said in a low voice and then added in a louder voice, "Let us in!"

"The shop of the blind potter? What's that? No, no. And you're not Blygen's guards! Go away!" The old man tried to close the door.

But Feirek had his foot and shoulder in the way of it. "This is the one, Worul, and you know it! If you don't let us in, we'll tell everyone in Adnor. You'll be sorry!"

At that the old man hesitated. "It's not the shop of the blind potter," he said stubbornly. "At least not now. Maybe once it was. Or maybe you see where it once was. I don't know. Now it's a shop of rags and bones. Shards and mullock. Bits and pieces of things left from no one knows where."

"The time has come to let their history through the door. Let us in." Feirek forced the door open a little farther.

Trembling, the old man gave way. Arela, Keld, and Elylden, pulling Thosstoe with her, followed Feirek into the dingy shop.

The old man eyed the dog with terror.

19

Small and grimy, the shop was filled with nothing that was not broken or tattered. Mugs without handles, handles without tools, harnesses with straps missing, cracked plates, torn blankets, rugs worn through, legless benches, boots without heels, split bellows—everything from rusted nails to half of a huge yoke for oxen all muddled together on shelves and floor.

Worul backed slowly through the room, protesting at every step.

"There!" Feirek pointed.

It was a potter's wheel, tilted, the base broken. Worul's wrinkled and veined hand brushed the powder of clay and dust into a tiny heap. As if that too must be kept, he picked it up and rubbed it between trembling thumb and forefinger.

"If this was his wheel, it's all that's left of him."

"What was his name?" Elylden asked. She would know if Anna's hands had touched it.

"The potter's? Who knows? Two hundred years ago he died."

Elylden looked steadily at him. Lying old rag-picker! He was as crumpled and broken as everything in his shop. She would learn about him as she was learning about others. How little they knew! How little they could do! She could make that old man smooth the powdered clay back over the wheel as the potter had left it two hundred years ago!

She watched the shaking hand move across the wheel, sprinkling and spreading and smoothing the clay. See? And Anna said she couldn't look out for herself!

She knew so much more than she had yesterday! This land was not empty as she had first thought it. It had more than men playing silly games with little dotted cubes. It had something much stronger, unlike anything there ever was at Wode Nen. It was the force on the river, more frightening than the burning of their cottage. She must be careful never to meet it. Not yet. Not until she was at least as old as Keld. She would tell Thosstoe about it.

Elylden gazed at the wheel and let the sense of it come to her. It was of the old ones. It had felt rain and wind. Flaming trees of burning forests had fallen upon it. It had endured the time of the giants and of the Wizards. It had been chipped and ground away by the hands of men and had turned and turned at their bidding. Now it rested. *Eternal patience of waiting stone.*

Had Anna's hands touched it? The more she looked at

it, the more she felt Anna's presence. She was not far away! She would come soon and take them to a better place. They must wait for her in the potter's shop. Waiting . . . It would be hard to learn the patience of stone. Even Keld would find that hard to do. But Anna should come by tomorrow.

While they waited she would notice everything. She would hide what she knew, keep it on the chain beneath her collar, or in her pocket or her shoe. She could hide it between her shoulder blades or in her throat or behind her eyes. Unlike her brother, she would know if someone touched it. She need never be afraid. She knew more than anyone here! Her lips curved as she glanced again at the old man.

Eyes narrowed, Worul was watching her brother.

Keld looked with a mixture of dismay and curiosity at the wheel. Was this the end of his journey to Adnor, his promise to his mother fulfilled? He had found the shop of the blind potter. He was free to leave this wretched town and seek the Knights of Ahln. The boy could not resist stretching out his hand to touch the heavy chipped stone surface.

The old man grasped his wrist with unexpected quickness.

"Where is the ring?" he whispered hoarsely.

"It . . . What ring?" he asked pulling away.

"Blygen's ring!" The old man thrust his face toward the boy. "Ten pieces of gold for finding the fair-haired boy who stole it!"

"That's why we're here," Feirek said. "Every fair-haired boy in the town will be in Blygen's dungeons. This boy is the son of a friend and has no ring. I'm looking after him. We need some changes made."

The old man grunted and peered suspiciously at Feirek.

"We'll change the color of his hair and find rags for him. Quick! We have to go from here sooner than now."

"And me?" Elylden asked.

"We have to stay together," Keld said at the same time.

"We'll see to you. Now, hurry, because they're looking house to house." Feirek took Worul by the arm. "If they find a fair-haired boy here you'll go with him to Blygen's dungeon."

"What is there in it for me?"

Feirek drew a handful of coins from his pocket and shook them. The old man shrugged his shoulders and, with mouth turned down even more, led them to a small room behind the shop. There he produced a basin, filled it with water from a jug, and began searching on a dusty shelf covered with bottles, crocks, and vials.

"Hurry!" Feirek said impatiently, his eyes snapping.

At last Worul found what he wanted and emptied the contents of a small bottle into a basin of water.

While Feirek doused Keld's head in the dark liquid, Arela gathered up Elylden's long hair at the nape of her neck. "I'm sorry," she murmured as she took quick scissors to it. She held out the long tresses before Elylden's startled eyes, then turned to the old man. "You can sell this. Good hair comes dear. The ladies of Blygen's court . . ."

"No!" Elylden cried. "You mustn't! Burn it! Please burn it!"

Arela was startled. "All right, if you say, but it's good money thrown away!" She pushed it into a small iron stove.

"It's not burned. There's no fire. Please, set tinder to it!"

"I don't see why all the fuss!" Arela exclaimed.

"Burn it!" Feirek commanded, his fingers on the nape of Keld's neck as he held the youth's dripping head over the basin.

Arela knelt before the stove and struck flint and steel for a spark. Smoking, the hair hissed, frizzed, and curled. The old man winced.

The woman turned to Elylden. "I'll trim it a bit more even."

Dark wisps appeared on the floor. Elylden carefully gathered them and threw them into the stove, watched them twist, then stirred the charred mat with a stick of kindling until no sign of hair was left.

"Now then." Arela took off her own kerchief and bound Elylden's head with it. "That takes care of that. Next you'll change into other clothes." She went to the shop and returned a few moments later with a sack. She opened the bundle and drew out what looked to Elylden to be no more than tatters.

"There's no help for it," the woman said gently. "If it's rags or your life, I'm sure you know which counts the most."

Elylden nodded and undid her frock.

In five minutes time she turned to Keld.

"Your eyes, Elyl," Keld murmured. "I shall always know your eyes."

Elylden nodded. Keld too—his eyes . . . There would never be a thing that could change them!

Arela stuffed their discarded clothes into the sack and carried it back to the shop.

"You know nothing of this at all," Feirek said to the old man.

"No," he grumbled. "But what more do I get for not knowing?"

"You get—" Feirek began, when there was a loud knock at the door.

"Open in the name of Blygen!" a voice cried. "Open before we break it down!"

"You get a pair of young ones to sort your rags," Feirek said between his teeth. "And two customers buying from you or you're dead!" He pushed Keld and Elylden into the shop as the old man hobbled to the door. "On your knees, and no talking!" he snapped, scooped up a pile of rags, and dumped them in front of them. "Sort them into ragged and less ragged!"

He moved quickly to Arela's side and picked up a tattered dress.

"So it ain't good enough for you!" he sneered as the door flew open. "Who do you think you are, the queen o' the sun and the moon?"

20

ickering and shouting, Feirek and Arela went out
the door.

Feirek poked his head back in. "I'll be back,
old man. I'll get what I want when there's no too-good-
for-the-lord's-court, la-di-da lady to give me blether." He
slammed the door.

The guards followed soon after.

"I'll not have you telling the street you're here," the
old man growled. "You'll stay hid till they come for you.
Get to the rags."

They sorted rags in the murky, ill-smelling room.
When someone rattled the door they crept beneath a table
heaped with broken chairs. Worul, terrified of the dog, let
Thosstoe into the alley. He would have left him there, but
the dog began clawing the door from the hinges.

That night the old man locked and barred the two
doors, front and back. He slept with the key on a chain
around his neck.

The next day they waited for Feirek to return. He didn't.

The grasping old man, the dirt and the disorder . . . Keld rubbed the grime from a spot in the greased skin of the narrow window and saw that the filth and slovenliness were not only in the shop. The street was choked with refuse and running with rats. Ragged children fought over a crust dropped in the gutter. He watched a palsied old woman, a young man with one leg—whoever came and went through the doors opposite the rag shop. Anna had never spoken of such!

"Don't look," Elylden told Keld. "You'll be sick." She huddled against the potter's wheel and talked to Thosstoe.

The third day Feirek came looking for a lamp wick. Keld crawled from beneath the table. Feirek brushed him off. "Get back where you came from. I'll find what I want myself, boy."

A second man came in and snooped and nosed, then followed Feirek when he left. Keld looked into the street, but Worul was at his side.

"Sit yourself at your rags," he hissed. "Don't never speak to your friend or you go into Blygen's hands. The chit and your friend too."

Feirek had whispered a quick promise: *We'll get you away as soon as we can. Be patient.*

Keld clenched his fist. He could not be patient much longer.

"How do we know Feirek will come for us?" he muttered to Elylden. "We'll leave, find our way from Adnor. Who's to stop us?"

"No. We have to wait a little longer," she said.

Pay attention to what she tells you.

The boy ground his teeth, angry with the old man for being what he was, angry with Feirek for leaving them there, angry with Elylden for insisting they stay. He was angry with Anna for sending them here and with the Knights of Ahln for having let him see them. Most of all, he was furious with himself for not knowing what to do.

Tomorrow he would insist! Why wait? It was as simple as that.

Keld half-turned from the window when he saw people in the street scatter, run for doors, open and slam them behind them. A troupe of riders clattered into the lane led by a gray-faced youth. A knife in his belt, a whip in his hand, his head turned from side to side.

To ride at the head of armed men! Keld envied him. The youth pointed his whip and flicked it. There was a cry. Another rider leaped from his horse and dragged a cowering boy from a doorway. He was thrown into a cart that followed the riders, and in two minutes all were gone.

Keld backed from the window and sat down, his face in his hands. He would never forget the gloating face of the rider as he used the whip.

"You see how it is?" Worul was at his shoulder. "They'll look here every day now. You're lucky that weren't you. Keep from the window."

Glaring at every scrap and tatter, Keld prowled through the shop.

That was when he found it—the ladder nailed to the wall, not broken like those piled against it but reaching to the ceiling. Above it was the outline of a square cut into the roof. He found a candle end.

That night, Elylden asleep, Keld stood under the sky and looked over a maze of roofs. Where was the river, the bridge over it that would take them from the dark, silent town? Tall houses blocked his view. Cautiously he made his way from one roof to the next, and to the one beyond. It was almost morning when he returned and crept under the table.

He woke to find Elylden bending over him.

"What's wrong?" she asked.

"Nothing," he said, knowing that he would explore every night until he found a way out of this miserable labyrinth.

When he returned the third morning Elylden was waiting for him.

"I'll go with you tonight."

"No. I'll find the way first. Then we'll go."

Her answer surprised him. "All right. I have to wait anyway."

"Why?"

"Because I do."

The sixth night as he peered over a roof edge, he heard a whisper.

"What are you doing?"

He whirled. Staring at him were a boy and a girl, small, ragged, scraggy-haired, faces smudged, eyes narrow with suspicion.

"I'm looking for the end of the town," he said.

"There's no end," the boy said. "It just goes around."

"Alios 'ud know. Could he trust him?" The girl pointed at Keld.

"If he don't, he'll put him out to the dogs. You want to ask Alios? I'm Nichil. She's Malkin."

"I'm Terach." Keld followed them across roofs and down a crumbling stair to a hut where four boys and two girls crouched around a brazier.

"This is Terach," Nichil said. They made room.

"Where's Alios?" Malkin asked when they were settled.

"He's gone."

A small whine came from Malkin. Her mouth closed tight, her arms hugged across her chest, she began to rock forward and back.

"Don't cry, Malkin!" the tallest boy ordered sharply.

Malkin made no more sound, but her face was contorted. Tears streaked her cheeks and she continued to rock. The others stared at the few embers in the iron pot. The youth, Parso, looked at Keld.

"Alios was going for a story. We told him we seen someone following Feirek. We could wait a night. But he went. They caught him."

"Feirek?" Keld was startled at hearing his name. "You know him?"

"Everybody does. Sometimes he helps. Alios got stories from him."

"What happened to Feirek?"

The boy shrugged. "I don't know."

Keld's heart sank.

"Do you know stories?" a girl asked in a flat voice.

"Yes." Keld nodded.

"Tell us one."

Malkin swayed back and forth, back and forth. Keld closed his eyes. The sound of Anna's voice, her words came to him.

"First was the time of the ancient ones . . .

The time of the giants. *"Some grew crafty, but none was wise . . ."*

He looked up to see eyes fixed upon him. How silent they were! Just as he used to be with Anna's telling.

"Third was the time of the wise ones, the Wizards . . . the beloved of the stars . . . One with the world, and one with each other they cherished what was precious . . .

Suddenly Anna's voice was gone. An awareness of time filled him.

Keld leaped to his feet. "I have to go back! Show me the way!"

"You'll come tomorrow night?"

"Yes, yes!" Elylden—alone with Worul!

They ran over the roofs until Keld recognized a tilted chimney. Relieved, he hugged Nichil briefly.

"Tomorrow night. Here!" he whispered, then turned and ran even faster, leaping from roof to roof. The stars were fading as he pulled the square of wood back into place above the ladder.

The next night ten ragged children waited. The third night the hut was crowded. Malkin sat on Keld's knees to hear of the powers of the Wizards and the Women of the Nedoman. The fourth night Keld told of the deeds of the Knights of Ahln.

Nichil leaned forward. "The Knights of Ahln—they're not like Blygen's guards?"

"No! Never!"

"Could I be one?" the boy asked. "Could I? A Knight of Ahln?"

Startled, Keld looked at the urchin. Thin-chested, large-eyed, dirty. He saw the Knights coming from between the two giant pines, tall, stately. The awe he had felt, the yearning, the ache to ride with them!

Keld stared at the small boy whose eyes were pleading, hopeful and hopeless at once. A tattered, starving beggar child. Nothing farther from . . . Suddenly Keld burned from his cheekbones to his ankles. His look passed to the faces of the others. Eyes of want. Girls, boys, dirty, ragged, hungry, as he was—in the belly. But deeper, a second hunger . . .

Like a sudden leaping of fire, another sense opened.

His eyes returned to Nichil's. Keld reached out to touch his face.

"Why not?"

21

t night they searched, Keld on his knees at the roof's edge, Parso beside him.

"Shhh! They're out with Blygen's dogs!"

Malkin, gnawing at her finger. "Last night they kilt Joggis."

A pain like a knife through Keld.

"Maybe they kilt the boy with the ring and threw him in the river."

"No. They'd have the ring then. They've not stopped looking."

Fire over the roofs. Parso: "I saw 'em set torches to it."

At last, the bridge. But the gates were closed and there were guards. Nichil's shoulders lifted. "Unless you want to swim. But nobody can't climb the wall on the other side."

Keld ground his teeth. Dogs . . . guards . . . walls . . . Blygen . . . Sirdde . . .

During the day some came so often to the shop that Keld and Elylden did not hide from them—a palsied old woman who could pick up nothing without dropping it, a gaunt young woman looking for a piece whole enough to wrap around the runny-nosed baby on her hip, an ancient, hunched cripple pawing again through what he had pawed through yesterday, handling every object on a shelf of trash, never buying.

Worul's eyes had narrowed when he first came in. "I don't know him. Watch him, boy. He's come to steal."

Keld never saw him steal. "Is he a thief?" he asked Elylden.

She shook her head. "I don't know. I don't think so."

"What does he tell you?"

"He doesn't talk."

"I don't mean in words. I mean . . . you know."

"I know. He picks things up off shelves and feels them. It's all there is. Shapes. Pins or broken boxes or rusty keys or old shoes."

"Is he like Pareth's nephew? What Anna said—simple?"

"I don't know." She frowned.

"He must be." Keld stopped watching him.

Another who came every day was the hag Jejur, whose words whistled through broken teeth. She and Worul gossiped and complained about 'young ones.'

He told her, "I'm trainin' two myself. One of each."

She told him, "They shay the boy had a shishter, so Loughat'sh collecting little girlsh now. Shirdde thinks she'll find Blygen's ring that way. I've lost my Bidgie and my Raggin to him, the shlimy weasel! It's bad for a boy to be took by Loughat. Worshe for a girl. Ye'll not feed yersh long. When ye want to be shut of 'em, I could ushe another girl."

Keld could stand no more. They would risk the bridge. "Elyl, I know how . . ."

She was staring at the potter's wheel. "Shh."

"What is it?"

"Something says . . ." She shook her head and bent to comb the dog.

"Never mind what it says. We have to go. I know where . . ."

She put her hand to her lips. "No. We have to wait."

"I can't! Not anymore! I know the way!"

"Arela says soon. Please? Just one day? Please? Please?"

Arela? He must have been asleep! He would have asked about Feirek! Keld rubbed his hands on his breeks. Anger, despair, and boredom!

"No. Today after the guards have gone through."

It was almost twilight before the clattering of Blygen's guards was heard. The last doors opened and closed quickly. Worul was on his way to bar the door when it burst open and a child ran in.

Worul snatched the small girl. "You don't hide here! Out!"

But Keld was beside him and twisted his hands from her arms. "Bar it, old man!" He pushed the child ahead of him to the back of the shop and behind the heap of boxes, pieces of iron, broken stools, and table legs, the mound of clutter he had added to their hiding place.

There was a pounding on the door, Worul's cry—"I'm opening!"—a stamping of feet, the sound of thrown objects, the smashing of crockery.

"She come through! She come through. But she ain't be mine!" Worul cried. "She come through and run out the back!"

Pressed between him and Elylden, the child clutched Keld's sleeve, her fingers like little claws. He could feel her bones through her scant rags, a thin bit of a girl whose terrified stillness was like that of a stalked animal. She hid with them until it was dark.

"Tomorrow, Elyl."

Elylden bent down. Her head on his knees, she cried.

But in the morning Worul unlocked the door. "Here!" he called. "There's nobody don't know about you now. Jejur needs you." He pushed them into the street, shut and locked the door behind them.

"Thosstoe!" Elylden cried, pulled at the door, beat on it with her fists. "He's asleep!"

"Now, now!" An ancient, stooped, and toothless woman stopped at the recess to peer at them. "You don't want that door open! There's creebles and glockies in there who'll eat the skin off your toes!"

"Bah!" Jejur hobbled across the street. "You're off your button, Mickle. Get to your housh before the real glock-iesh get you!" She shoved the old woman aside and turned to Keld.

"Do you hear 'em? They're on their way. Thish way, before the brutsh of Lord High Blygen come by, or you'll feel Loughat'sh whip and he'll serve you both to Lady Shirdde for dinner."

At the name of Blygen, Elylden turned from the door.

"My dog!" she cried.

"A dog'll find hish way by hish nose, which is more than you can, ye little shcragget. March you both quick or ye'll be shorry."

Jerking her head toward Keld, the old woman seized Elylden's arm and pushed her across the street, down steps, through a door, and announced, "Here'sh Tritt and Shcragget. Come to town lookin' for gold."

22

A dozen hungry-eyed children pressed together on benches and floor. Some grinned like foxes, some were sullen, some sat with eyes fixed on nothing.

Jejur threw a sack on the table. Two of the taller children snatched it, undid the drawstring, and dumped the contents on the table. The rest scrambled for crusts, bits of moldy cheese, and shriveled carrots. In half a minute the table was cleared. One small girl sucked her fingers and whimpered.

"You got to be quicker, Magget! What have you got fer me?"

The child held out her hand and uncurled her fingers.

The hag snorted and took the small coin. "Who give it ye?"

"I foun' it on the cobbles," mumbled the child.

"You got to get your fingersh in a pocket." Jejur leaned toward Magget and wiggled her fingers. "Ain't Grolly taught you how?"

A sullen boy wiped his mouth with the back of his hand. "She don't come high enough for a pocket."

"Then she got to grow. Give her your bread."

But Grolly had stuffed the last of his into his mouth.

Muttering, Jejur searched her pockets, came up with a crust, and handed it to Magget. "Don't shay I never done nothing for you. What have the rest of you brought?"

The children again gathered around the table. There were coins, a small gold chain, a dented silver thimble, a string of glass beads.

The hag grunted, counted the coins, and swept them from the table into a pouch. She tucked the chain away with the thimble and beads and then turned to Elylden. "You've had your hand in a pocket?"

"No."

"Ye'll learn, won't you dearie."

Jejur turned her small eyes on Keld. "What can ye do?"

"I can milk a cow."

"Why did you come away from milk and cheezh?"

"I thought to learn a craft," he said.

"Ha! Better learn to be crafty. Now the shtreet's clear, sho out you go. Dregg, take Shcragget. Teach her how you earn your way in Adnor. You, Grolly, take Tritt. Ye'll learn quick, boy," she said to Keld, "or ye'll lie in Blygen's dungeon aside the boy with the ring."

The day was almost over when Grolly held up the pouch. "It's the best I done today. You seen how. A bump in a crowd and it's Jejur's. Wup!" He pushed Keld into a doorway. "He almost seen us. Now you do one."

Keld protested. "I can't take a man's purse! Steal his work!"

Grolly snorted. "Didn't I learn by sweat an' beatin's an' goin' hungry? You'll have that tonight if you don't do it. There's one! He'll never know who took it!"

Grolly pushed Keld against a man who had just returned his money pouch to his pocket, the string hanging loose. But Keld had seen something else and stooped to pick it up.

"You dropped this," he said, touching the arm of the portly man.

"Did I now?" The man looked with round eyes at the boy. "And you're giving it back to me, are you? So why didn't you keep it, eh, eh? You're ragged enough!"

Between the man going on and Grolly hissing him for being a fool, Keld didn't know what to say except, "I saw it fall."

"So you did!" The man took Keld's arm firmly and, huffing, pulled him along. "That's news! Come along, boy."

"I didn't do anything wrong! Let me go!" Where was Grolly? He would never find his way to Jejur's cellar without him!

The stout man did not let go his arm. "Why? An honest boy is hard to come by. If I've found one, I'll keep him. Hmmpf. See there? Blygen's men watching us! Don't fuss or they'll take you for a thief and you'll dance on the gallows tomorrow."

It was enough to quiet Keld for a moment. They rounded a corner.

"Here!" He pushed Keld into a small carriage, climbed in, tossed a coin to the boy who held the horse, and shook the reins.

Frantic now, Keld turned to him. "I have to go back!"

The man pulled out a handkerchief, wiped his brow, and blew his nose. "Why? Where?"

"I've lost my sister! She's so young! She'll be afraid. How can I find her? I don't know the way back!"

"Back to where? Why don't you know?" The man turned his eyes on Keld.

"We've just come to Adnor. I don't know the town. We were together and then she was gone. I have to find her!"

It was true. When they left the hag's cellar, he had planned to go to the bridge, but Grolly was always between him and Elylden. For a short way the girls were just behind him, but Grolly, pushing Keld ahead of him, had ducked into an alley. Keld turned back at once, but there was no sign of Elylden or Dregg and Magget in the crowded street.

"They've gone to do their bit. Dregg'll bring 'er in tonight," Grolly said impatiently. "You stick with me or you'll not find the way."

True. Keld was certain only of the last three turns they

had made. If he found the street he was not sure he would know Jejur's door or the shop of the blind potter either, for he had scarcely seen the outside of it. He looked in dismay at the unfamiliar wide street the horse and cart now turned into.

"What does she look like?" asked the man.

"She's small and ragged and wears a kerchief around her head."

"Harrumph! Like very other moppet in the gutter. She'll soon enough be in bad hands. Adnor's no place to lose a little sister."

"Then take me to the street of the blind potter!" Keld cried.

"*Where?*" The man's eyes were suddenly wary.

Elylden watched Dregg tilt her head to one side, hunch her shoulder, and curl her fingers. Twice during the morning a coin was dropped in the crippled-looking hand. Otherwise she was ignored, or a threatening look sent her scuttling way. Magget, sucking her fingers, big-eyed and fearful, plodded wearily behind Dregg.

Elylden wondered at the bright heaps of cloth and the glint of brass and tin in the open shops. She listened to the cries of vendors and sniffed the unfamiliar odor of strange foods cooking.

Anna had told her to notice everything, hadn't she?

Anna! It had been so hard waiting for her and she hadn't come! Feirek and Arela hadn't come for them either. But Keld knew the way to the bridge now. Anna must want them to come to her. They would go through the Valley of Hune to Wode Nen and up to the Crags of Ahln. She would tell Anna how much she had noticed and how bad it was. Anna would tell them they could stay with her forever!

The three children moved slowly through the crowded street. Elylden was not about to beg, nor did she fancy lifting a pouch from a pocket the way she saw a boy do it—the one who turned too fast, tripped, and fell. The pouch flew from his hand. Only she saw little Magget scoop it up, thrust it into her pocket, and put her fingers back in her mouth.

Dregg turned to Elylden.

"You got to beg, Scragget. It ain't fair makin' me do it all."

"All right. That man—he'll give you something." Elylden pointed.

"How do you know?"

"Try him."

Dregg sidled up to the thin, sallow fellow, the least promising looking of anyone. "A penny, mister?" she asked in her husky voice.

Beside her, Magget by the hand, Elylden screwed up her face. Tears came to her eyes. "For Dorie, Mister? She got a fever."

The stranger looked down at the ragged threesome, muttered, and dropped a handful of coins into Dregg's palm.

Dregg stared at the unexpected amount.

"Thanks, mister." Elylden sniffed, rubbed her hand across her eyes.

Already wondering at his own generosity, the man lifted the stick he carried. "Go on, you little beggars!"

They scurried away. Dregg stopped in a doorway to tie the coins in her kerchief. "Who's Dorie?" she asked.

"A pony," Elylden said. "She's dead now."

"Eeeh." Dregg wrinkled her nose. She couldn't believe her luck. "You know somebody else to ask?"

"No." Elylden decided she had done enough for today.

"Come on then." Dregg pulled at her arm. "There was a fire a couple nights ago. Maybe it's cool now and we can find something. Everybody'll be looking. Sometimes you find something in the ashes."

The smell of smoke and burned rubble hung in the air of the narrow, twisting way. Elylden chewed her underlip. The street was familiar.

"There." Dregg pointed.

A crowd was watching men with rakes sift through rubble.

Dregg turned to a boy as ragged as herself. "Them's Blygen's men. What're they looking for?" she asked.

"They're looking for Blygen's ring," the boy said.

"How do they know it's there?"

"They say as Scroot told that the boy with the ring went in there."

Scroot! Elylden stooped suddenly to pick an object from the rubble.

"Hey!" one of the men shouted. "What you got there?"

She held it out in her open palm. He turned it over, dropped it, and went back to work.

Elylden picked it up again. Her eyes went from the shard of pottery in her hand to the other houses along the street. This was the house Feirek had brought them to. Arela's house.

"Was the folk in it burned?" someone asked.

"Must 'a been," answered another. "No one come out the door."

"Why should they? The guards was waitin'."

"They've found no bones," argued a third.

"Not yet," the second man said. "You wait. They will."

Elylden stood very still. She had no sense of bones. Arela and Feirek would have gone down through the hole in the floor, wouldn't they? Anna? Why didn't you come! I waited so long!

It was hard not to cry. When they were back with Jejur she would tell Keld they must go at once. Feirek might not come after all. Adnor was a bad place! Her brother knew that, but it was worse than he knew. Again she fought back tears.

Worse than she knew only a minute ago, she found as they turned into the wide street they had crossed after she lost Keld. For coming toward them down that street were horses pulling a closed carriage. In the carriage was something so terrible that Elylden could scarcely heed Dregg's warning to get off the street. She pressed herself against a wall, closed her eyes, and covered her face with her hands.

She heard the cry, "Sirdde! Sirdde!"

She shuddered at the name and then she heard the command as the carriage rattled by. It roared and shrieked in her ears and made the wall behind her shake.

"Fetch me that girl!"

Her legs trembling, Elylden turned and ran around the corner into another street. She knew at once that it led to that of the blind potter. Only a little way and she would be safe.

She ran as she had never run in her life, but it was not fast enough. There were steps behind her and someone seized her arm.

23

ou! Come with me!" He grasped her arm more tightly. He was older than Keld, a little taller, his face a waxy gray, his eyes small.

"What do you want?" Elylden hit at him and tried to pull away.

"You!" he said, leering, his lips drawing back from his teeth.

"Get away from me! I won't go with you!" She kicked him.

Suddenly the youth twisted her arm around behind her and then threw her to the ground. "Get up and come on," he ordered, "or you'll have worse than that!"

At that moment a cart pulled by a smartly trotting horse and carrying a stout man and a boy turned into the street.

Keld knew at once that it was Elylden. He leaped from the cart and threw himself at the youth. "Let her go!" he shouted.

It was the rider he had seen—the one with the whip. Keld was aware of the knife in the other's hand and that it was slashed at him, but he was so furious that he felt no fear. He caught the wrist. The gray-faced youth kicked and Keld grabbed his boot, twisted his leg, threw him down, and flung himself on him. Pushing his face into the muck of the gutter, Keld sat on the youth's shoulder and wrenched the knife from him.

"I'll let you up, but you'll have to run to stay alive!" Again he rubbed the youth's face in the mud, then jumped to his feet.

The other youth too scrambled to his feet. He stood with his back against a door and stared wildly at Keld. People drifted from doorways.

"Run!" Keld shouted. "Before I kill you!" Holding the knife by the tip of the blade he flung it with all of his strength. The knife grazed the youth's head and the blade sank deep into the wood.

The youth ran.

Elylden huddled on the street, her fist to her lips, her eyes wide. Keld seized her wrists and pulled her to her feet. With a rage in him that he never imagined he could feel, he glared at the crowd around them.

"Loughat!" He heard a voice. "It was the Lady Sirdde's Loughat!"

"Make way!" Keld ordered and dragged his sister behind him as the crowd parted silently.

"Why did you . . . I could have . . ." she gasped.

"No you couldn't!" he snapped. "Not here. Never here!"

"Where . . . ?"

"We're leaving."

He had taken only twenty steps when he felt a hand on his shoulder. He whirled. It was the old cripple from Worul's shop.

"What do you want?" Keld growled.

"Where are you going?" the man asked.

"Away from here. Over the bridge as fast as we can!"

"You'll never go alive that way. Come, I'll see you safe."

There was a look in the man's eyes that Keld could have trusted without question a month ago. Now he hesitated.

"Hurry!" the man urged.

Keld nodded. The old man pointed and, hobbling faster than the boy could believe possible, led the way through the twisting alleys. In a short time he pulled open a door and motioned to them to enter. Pushing Elylden before him, Keld stepped into the dark room. The man closed the door, and Keld felt him brush past. In a moment a lamp flared.

It was a small room furnished with a cot, a chair, and a table.

Keld's look came to the hunchback. Again—what? He knew him from Worul's rag shop, but this went deeper, came from some other place.

"I've seen you. I . . . I don't know your name," he stammered.

"Call me Zirawd," said the man. His voice was unexpectedly low. He motioned toward Elylden. "She had better rest."

Elylden was shaking. Her face white, she leaned against Keld. He helped her to the cot and Zirawd covered her with a blanket. Keld put his hands over her clenched and trembling fists.

"Something hot for her to drink," the man said, and taking a small pan from a shelf, he filled it from a pitcher and set it above the lamp.

"Now we'll tend to that." Zirawd nodded toward Keld's arm.

Keld looked down. His shirtsleeve, soaked with blood, hung over his wrist. He stared at it, wondering what it meant. He felt no pain.

Zirawd pointed to the chair beside the table. "Sit down. I'll cut away the sleeve and wash it so we can see the damage."

Keld did as he was told. His anger was dissolving. He wondered that such a fury dwelt in him, that he could do what he had done. Suddenly he too began to shake. He curled his fingers into fists, hugged his elbows against his sides, and clenched his teeth. He didn't want this old man to know . . . He watched as Zirawd sharpened a knife and then cut away the sleeve.

"It's not deep. It's already stopped bleeding. I'll bind it."

The water had heated. The man took a cup from the shelf, poured an amber liquid into it, and added the water. He roused Elylden.

Supporting her with his arm, he forced her to drink. She coughed and sputtered and then lay back. Zirawd drew the blanket around her shoulders and came to sponge the dried blood from Keld's now throbbing arm. The boy was surprised at his quickness and care. Nothing about him made sense. After knotting a cloth around the wound the man again mixed a drink and handed it to Keld.

As he sipped, heat spread through his body. He had never felt so limp. Keld put his head down on his arms. As the room darkened, he heard the man's words: "I believe I hear your friend . . ."

Someone was calling him. "Keld! Keld!"

He raised his head. Feirek's face was close to his. "Are you all right? You look like death turned thrice around!"

Keld was aware of a fierce pulsing in his arm.

"I saw the end of it," Feirek went on. "Only I wasn't close enough to . . . Tell me where you learned to throw a knife like that!"

"In an oat field," Keld said. He rested his arms on the table and closed his eyes, fearing he would be sick.

"Still the peasant boy? Don't lie to me!" Feirek snapped.

"I used to throw it at a fence post," the boy mumbled, "at a knot in . . . the wood." He was glad to lose himself again in darkness.

★ ★ ★

Elylden opened her eyes and looked at the ceiling. There was so much to think about. The worst was . . . Tears gathered in the corners of her eyes and ran hot down the sides of her face into her hair.

Keld. First his voice had changed, then his eyes. It was her fault. She had been so sure there was nothing she could not take care of. Now she knew something could happen before she had time to understand it. She turned on her side, blinked, and blinked again. There was a face before her, eyes looking anxiously into her own.

"Thosstoe!" she cried and threw her arms around his neck. He licked the salty wetness off her ear.

"Elylden?" Keld sat down on the cot beside her. His face was pale and his mouth tight and hard as she had never seen it.

She could not stop the tears from coming again. Elylden sat up and pressed her face against his shoulder. He put his arm around her.

"You're safe now, Elyl. He'll never touch you."

She wouldn't have had to look into his face, but she did. He wouldn't have had to say it, but he did.

"If he ever tries, I'll kill him."

The sadness started. Nothing would ever be the same. His voice was different and his eyes were different and his mouth was different. Even the feel of his arm, hard and tight around her, was different.

She must stop dreaming of going through the Valley

of Hune, of finding Anna behind the Crags of Ahln and telling her how well she could look after herself, how well she could look after her brother because there was so much he didn't know. Because Keld knew something about this country that she didn't know. It made him part of it now. He would never go back, so neither could she. For however much she might want Anna, how could she go without Keld?

She closed her eyes tightly against new tears. Please, Anna, she begged silently. Please, please, please . . .

24

on't cry, Elyl. Why shouldn't she come? Anna can go anywhere!"

"Then why isn't she here now?"

Keld smiled a little and mopped at the tears on her face. "I suppose she has her reasons."

Elylden nodded and tried to laugh, but still could only cry.

While Keld tried to comfort her, Feirek spoke with Zirawd.

"They'll be searching twice as hard now! There's not the space of a cat's paw print that won't be combed. Where can we hide them?"

Zirawd poured a drink for the young man. "They won't come here." He set the cup before him. "Why are you trying to hide these two of all the young ones beaten, killed, or seized for worse every day?"

"I've tried now and again to shield a child," Feirek muttered.

"Not like this. Why these two?"

Feirek hesitated. He sipped the drink, and his look went to Keld and Elylden. "Because at the Rusty Crow, I felt . . . because, well, there's only so much you can stand. And the ring . . . I don't know! When he asked for the street of the blind potter—what did they know of words we use? The story of Anna and the blind potter . . . hope." He scowled. "I have a sense of why. What I don't understand is Sirdde. What's new in a scoundrel not paying for his supper? The ring—looking for it the next day! It might be a piece of tin! Why does she want it?"

"Sirdde's reasons are her own," Zirawd interrupted. "Or perhaps they are the same as yours—she has a sense of something."

"Hah!" Feirek snorted.

"Your reasons? You mentioned hope."

"It's more than that. It's what's been forgotten. What no one dares admit existed. Is it honesty? Trust? Compassion? Beauty? They're all but lost now! We have only suspicion and fear. Anna—there was something fine then. We *know* it, though no one ever saw her. No one knows what she or the blind potter were, or what he taught her. For most, she's an old wives' tale. For us—a . . . a legend, an ideal.

"When that boy showed us the ring and said that Anna—his mother—had given it to him, something turned in everyone in that room. You could feel the air snap!" Feirek's voice grew lower.

"When he threw Loughat down—that vicious pick-thank of Lady Sirdde—I've seen what he's done to children! Do you know how long it's been since anyone dared lift a hand against Blygen's toad-eaters? Those watching, did you see their faces? Do you know what kind of fire that boy has started? I wish the knife had been two inches to the right!"

"That would have been too much," Zirawd said thoughtfully. "The Lady Sirdde would have had her revenge on all of Adnor."

"How would she know they buried him with the other dead of the day?"

"She would have known."

"Spies and toadies! But word goes to other ears than hers! What happened today is talk everywhere now. Hundreds like that boy and his sister have come to Adnor looking to Blygen for protection from marauders and killers. How did they know that the ones they flee are Blygen's own? That he seizes their land, and when they come here they have no way to live but by thievery? For that they're hanged."

Feirek rubbed his forehead. "Those of us who've tried to keep something alive from before, who've tried in some way to fight Blygen—even with words—we're being hanged too. What protection is a tunic against a sword, a collar against the hangman's noose, or memory against an axe! Do you know what despair is?

"That boy—he's the first to come to give us hope. To

defy one of Blygen's brutes openly. And the girl, to hear her say exactly what she thinks is like a drink of spring water to those of us choked on a running gutter of lies. Me—I'll risk my head for him and his sister."

Finding Zirawd's questioning eyes upon him, he returned the look defiantly. "Yes! I'll live by those words or die by them. If I live long enough to have children, they'll owe him their fealty as well!"

Feirek snorted and went on. "Zirawd . . . you're new here, aren't you? But you see how it is. Your face tells me you think mine may be a short life, don't you? Then what about yourself?"

Feirek leaned forward. "Why did *you* help them? You couldn't help yourself, could you? Everyone in that crowd felt the same thing. Oh, they'll start to wonder what to make of it. As it was with the ring—what was it? Sirdde's gift to Blygen, or something else? In *my* bones it was something else. Now that it's lost who'll ever know?"

"Lost?" Zirawd lifted his head and glanced toward Keld. "You've lost the ring?"

The question caught the boy's attention.

"I didn't lose it. It was stolen. But I don't need it. Not now. Not ever. What does it matter who I am or who my father was? I'll do what I have to do, earn my way, and look after my sister. All we need do is get away from Adnor. Find a village where . . ." He looked down at his hands and frowned. "She told me to learn a craft. To learn to shape clay. So I will. Better not to wear a ring when you work with mud. Anna took hers off when she worked with it."

"Did she! Well, perhaps with mud, yes. But there are different kinds of clays. Did she tell you which kind you were to shape?"

"I expected the blind potter to teach me," Keld said sullenly. "I'll find another craftsman—even one who can see will do."

"Ah! And the Knights of Ahln? You've given up looking for them?"

Keld sucked in his breath and lifted his eyes to the hunchback's face. How did he know about them? He glanced at Feirek, then back at Zirawd. The man did not seem to be mocking him. Another thing, Zirawd sat easily on the edge of the table, his back as straight as any man's, his face—younger? Yes, but—not exactly. What had it been before? He had never more than glanced at him! Now his whole look was different. He was straight, tall, eyes searching—as Anna's used to.

Keld swallowed.

"If I thought I could . . . I wanted . . . But there was no trace of them after the falls of Gresheen. No one here has seen them. People thought I was a fool to ask about them." He scowled again, beginning to grow angry. "It's just as well I lost them! They brought nothing but trouble. The ring too! Trouble for us and others! Elylden . . . Today, the man—whoever he was—if he hadn't brought me in the cart . . ."

His eyes went to his clenched fist. He did want the ring, but it was gone. He did want to know who his father was, but now he would never find out. He did want to join the Knights of Ahln, but never had they seemed so far away. What was it that really mattered?

He put his arm around his sister. "Anna said to take care of her. I couldn't even do that! If it weren't for a stranger I would have lost her too. The Knights of Ahln— why should they want me?"

"Keld?" Elylden's voice was small. She reached out.

His fingers crossed over hers. "Maybe I don't want to join them with spears and swords—even to defend," he said in a low voice. "There's nothing here to defend! It's all wrong. Maybe I want to do as Anna told me—if not shape clay, I don't know what. I want to get away from here to build . . . something!" Troubled, he tried to explain, as much to himself as to this now silent stranger.

"We've been locked in Worul's shop full of nothing but dregs and lees. I've seen nothing from the window but dregs and lees of people! Worul taking money for rags that could never be mended!" He looked up angrily, his voice rose. "When he pushed us out this morning I was never so glad in my life! We would find something clean, something whole! But what did I see?" He glared at Zirawd and then at Feirek.

"I saw houses that had been burned and never built again. Charred wood and rubble. Not just from yesterday, but from a year ago. Five years, more than that! I saw thieves going through other men's pockets. Children picking through refuse. Beggars sitting in doorways, mouths hanging open, no legs, twisted arms, mangled hands stretched out—it's summer now. Where do they go in the winter?

"Jejur's children, the food she brought them—they were glad for it!" Keld's throat closed up as he thought of the smell of baking loaves, the taste of honey and strawberries.

"Is this country so poor there's no food? I've been hungry and so has Elylden, but that little Magget! I've never seen anything so hungry! At home the wood rats were fat!"

His eyes burned with anger and shame. He brushed his sleeve across them. "I saw people afraid to speak, afraid to defend themselves when they were dragged off the street. Staris and Toseny talked of it, but I didn't know what it meant until I saw it." He glared at Feirek.

"Who is Blygen that he treats his people so? People cast off like the rot of Worul's shop! Who is this Lady Sirdde that she wants a ring somebody in a stinking pothouse saw a peasant boy wearing? They say she'll kill for it! Children! Yes! Where *are* the Knights of Ahln?" Now he challenged Zirawd. "If they're near, how can they let this happen? Yes, I *would* fight beside them, but how do you kill hunger with a sword? How do you kill cruelty? If I battled beside them, they would have to fight differently!"

Zirawd's eyebrows rose and Keld looked away. "I

don't want to be where the things I've seen can happen. I don't want to be in a place that's so shameful, that won't let anyone think or build or even live! To kill instead of keep!" He caught himself. "Anna—it's what she said. *Better to succor than slay.*" Frowning, he stared down at his clenched fist and muttered, "I would do that."

Neither Feirek nor Zirawd had a reply for his anger.

"Keld?" Elylden unfastened Thosstoe's collar and leash. She slipped her fingers along it and then held out her hand, palm up.

"Here's your ring."

Slowly Keld reached for it. Slowly he slipped it onto his finger.

"She told him not to give it, but she didn't tell me not to take it!" Elylden defended herself before the three pairs of probing eyes. "I had to, or she would have found us right away. But she would never feel Thosstoe wearing it. She would never even guess."

"Feel it? Guess? Who . . . ?" Keld asked.

"Eddris."

"Eddris! What has she to do with it? The greatest of the Women of the Nedoman! What are you talking about!" Keld stared at her.

"Anna told us never to say it backwards—the rune of regis arcanum," Elylden said. "I know why now. Because backwards is the wrong side of it. It's the wrong side for everything. It's of the opposites. Like Sirdde. Because that's what Sirdde is. It's Eddris. Backwards. Oh Keld, I can't pretend anyone worse!" There was fear again in her eyes, and tears. "She went past in the street and told that man to catch me! I couldn't stop him. I tried to run."

She brushed the tears away and looked from Keld to Feirek and then to Zirawd. There her gaze rested.

"Why wouldn't you ever talk to me in the rag shop?" she asked. "I knew you could tell me something. But you wouldn't even tell me your name. It isn't Zirawd at all, is it? And it's not Dwariz either. I tried that just now, very carefully, and it doesn't mean a thing!

"I've found out about everyone else, and I tried and tried to find out about you but I couldn't. Only that your name is something else. I won't call you anything that isn't yours. Please tell me what I should call you! Please?"

The man rose to his feet. He was indeed tall. There was no sign at all of his being crippled or hunchbacked. He took something from his pocket and, his dark eyes fixed upon Elylden, held it toward her. She slipped from the cot, went to him, and held up her open palm.

"A remembrance from Anna," he said and dropped into her hand a small object, a toy made of sticks with a bit of wool glued to it.

"Call me Stilthorn."

e's only fainted," Stilthorn murmured as he eased Feirek to the floor. "He'll come around in a minute. Here, a little cold water."

Feirek sighed and his eyelids quivered. He opened his eyes, stared an instant at the faces above him, groaned, and closed them again.

"Come, man," the Wizard said. "You've more courage in you than this! If there's anyone to fear, it's not one of us!"

"No, I don't believe it. I'm dreaming. There was something in that drink. It's a mockery, an illusion, an apparition!" Feirek muttered.

Seeing the same faces still before him, he sat up and held his head in his hands. "You're joking, teasing me. Tormenting me. You're lying!" He pushed himself to his feet and staggered to the chair.

Stilthorn smiled slightly. Keld watched Feirek with concern. When Elylden saw him get to his feet, her face cleared.

"I knew it! I knew!" She was ecstatic. "You're Stilthorn! You're my grandfather!"

Once more the room swirled around Feirek.

Consciousness began to return. He was first aware of
the murmur of voices. He lay limp. It was Staris, doubtless, and Toseny. Of course. Yes. Who else? Yet he dared
not open his eyes because they were not their voices. He
swallowed. Was he in his grave? No. He was on a cot.
This was not a winding sheet but a blanket. His fingers
trembled and he pulled his hand back beneath the cover.
He still dared not look.

The murmur sorted itself into words that began to
string themselves together, have meaning.

"Then she can't return? We'll never see her again?"

"Never." The depth of the voice brought gooseflesh to
Feirek's entire body.

"We knew that, really, didn't we Elyl? We knew! Never
mind. You can cry. Here, I . . ." The boy's voice broke.

Feirek could feel a stinging in his own eyes at the sound
of the little girl's sobbing. When it subsided, the youth's
voice came again.

"What can I do? How can I fight anyone as strong as
Eddris?"

"Your strength is her weakness."

"I don't know what my strength is," Keld said slowly.
"Elylden has Anna's. I don't. I take her word for what I
know she understands. Without her, I can't see beyond or
behind what lies in front of me."

"There are a thousand ways of seeing beyond and behind what lies before you. You have only to understand one—your own."

There was a time of silence. Stilthorn broke it.

"You want me to tell you what way that is, don't you? You want me to show you how, to help you."

"You see?" Keld cried. "You can read my thoughts! I can't read anyone's thoughts!"

"I don't read your thoughts, but your face. It takes no wizard to do that!"

At the word "wizard" Feirek shuddered.

"I have had more years of practice than you, but you can do it well enough," the man's voice went on. "Come now, didn't you see the look on your friend's face as he talked of you just a bit ago? He spoke of the people in the street, their faces. Didn't you see them too?"

"I saw only the red of fire."

"Your anger! Well well, that's a beginning. It will drive a man. But take care. The fire of anger can blind you when you most need to see clearly. Now you want to know what direction you must turn. I take it you want to run away to some kinder place and leave these people to the affectionate care of Sirdde and her consort, Blygen?"

"Run away? I never said that!" the boy answered hotly. "I . . ."

"Yes?"

The silence grew so long that Feirek opened his eyes and raised himself on an elbow.

Elylden had fallen asleep at the table, her head resting on her arms. The youth and the tall Wizard faced each other, eyes locked.

Words! If I only had words! A terrible need for them swept through Feirek. The boy and the man, the girl sleeping—the power that grew minute by minute in that small room.

How can I tell anyone of it? Feirek wondered. How can I even tell myself? How can I say that my body, from my throat to the soles of my feet, feels as if it would burst? That my eyes have grown wide as the rising moon, that my ears are ringing with the sound of a thousand clanging bells?

How can I make anyone believe that the light of that small lamp is as dazzling as the golden sheen of snow beneath the dawn, that it has melted away the wall and shows me the dark skies of the infinite!

How can I see the mountains of November, draped in damasked silver, float in the blue air? How can I behold the seas swirl up to stand in a mighty column waiting to rain their waters upon a desert earth whose plains are of copper and cliffs of brass? How do I know that when the waters fall they will resound like the clashing of giant arms upon the iron shield of forever?

And now . . . now . . . how is it I watch crystal stars fall from the velvet night into the outstretched hand of the Wizard and see them melt into his flesh? How do I know that the skies have stopped turning, and time has stopped its flow, that there is no heartbeat in the eternal?

How do I know anything but that my hair is standing on end?

The Wizard's fingers touched the boy's face. "You will do what you have to do, great-great-grandson of Benelf, grandson of Stilthorn, son of Anna."

Feirek cried out, closed his eyes, and covered his ears with his hands. When he looked again, the vision had faded. The room was small, the man a man, and the boy a boy.

Feirek found that he was able to draw air into his lungs. That he could hear the quiet breathing of Elylden. That his eyes were filled with tears and his mind empty of words.

26

"Well, poet, have you recovered your wits?" The Wizard turned his dark eyes on Feirek.

"My wits will never be the same," Feirek murmured.

"And your resolve?"

"Will never change."

The Wizard nodded. "Your kind is needed to speak to the mute anguish of these people who have been drenched in lies, beaten, and starved until they can think no thought of their own." His eyebrows came together. "Man! What a coming down this is from what he was, from what he might have been!"

"Of what he was and is and will be!" Feirek protested. "Many fight to speak aloud, many beg for learning, many set their lives against Blygen's brutality and die because of it."

"I'm glad to know, because all I've seen is ignorance and squalid poverty, man impoverished in both mind and body. There's no virtue in the show of wealth, but the beggary of Adnor denies the essence of man's spirit—or what it should be!"

"Of what it is, given a chance! Even without a chance!"

"I shall take your word, poet. You give me hope. I know it is not all by chance you find yourselves in the hands of one like Blygen. Part is bad luck—the strength of brutal invaders. But part is the fault of your people, your lack of diligence in knowing and protecting what is of value. The two have brought you to this misery.

"If it is as you say, bring together those who are of like mind. Give them this message. I cannot release you from Blygen. This is no longer my world. I cannot interfere with matters here. The cost of freedom and knowledge will be yours. Your battle will be hard fought. There will be suffering. You will need leaders to keep the fire of hope kindled through the winter, to prick and prod those who would remember Blygen's as a clement rule. That brutal lord will not fall gently. You must all fight hard with your swords!"

"I'm not much with a sword," Feirek muttered.

"You call yourself a poet? *Your* sword is your tongue! Why do you think Blygen stops it? Why do you think learning is kept from the children of Adnor? If poets do not speak to the horror of the corruption of the likes of Blygen, who wallow in a self-indulging obscenity of power while children starve in the streets, who will do it?

"As Sirdde is to Blygen, for she is worse than he and

whispers him on to greater cruelty, so you must be to your kind—with words! Mind to mind! Heart to heart! Those who use swords of steel run no greater risk than you! Urge them to use their weapons. If there is to be any justice, any decency in this Adnor, Blygen must be driven from here.

"But first Sirdde—Eddris must go. She is of other pith. Her power you cannot touch, nor can you succeed with Blygen while it stays. She belongs neither here nor in this time. Nor do I. She is my—our burden." He glanced at Keld and Elylden. "She would not be here but for them. We will draw her from this place. When she is gone, it will be for you to defeat Blygen. It is for us to . . . do what we can.

"Go now. Find those men whose fire has not been snuffed out. I hope you will kindle the spirit of all the people of Adnor so that they rise with you."

Feirek somehow found his feet beneath him. Stilthorn, his arm over the young man's shoulder, drew him to the door.

"I say good-bye to you for myself. I doubt I shall see you again. For my grandchildren . . ." He did not finish the sentence but opened the door. "Ah, it's morning! You'll be safe. Go to your friends. What is it that you say? Be of good heart? Yes. Those are the words."

"Our words. Yes. But you . . . your world . . ."

Stilthorn put his hands on the young man's shoulders and looked into his eyes. "I had always thought poets to be near that second world that walks close beside your own. But I see you fear more than love it."

"I . . . I might come to cherish it if I could see it from a safe distance," Feirek admitted. "But to be this close is more than I . . ." His voice trailed off.

The Wizard smiled. "Is its whisper too loud a roar for such tender ears? Yes, perhaps so, and doubtless with good reason. Good-bye, Feirek. May you and yours never kneel to the like of Sirdde."

The door closed behind him. Dazed, Feirek moved through the narrow alley and into another. He made several turns before he took note of where he was. Suddenly he thought of something he must ask. He turned back the way he had come. Yes, this was the street Parso had brought him to. Parso had seen even more of it than he had and told him of it blow for blow. What a grin he'd had for the rubbing of Loughat's face in the gutter!

There! He recognized the house on the corner. Yes, and that window across from him, he'd noticed that too. In fact, he knew the street well. Why must he prove it to himself? He hurried along until he came to the fourth door. It was the fifth he wanted, the one across from the tailor's shop. He was pleased that he remembered . . .

But there was no fifth door. There was a wall with no door, not even a window. Beyond was a pile of rubble— a row of houses and shops that had burned a year ago. Nothing more.

Feirek's throat tightened. He walked again to the corner and returned once more, pausing before the fourth doorway. As he stood there a man and woman came through it, looked hard at him, and then went on. The man glanced back.

Feirek wet his lips and crossed the alley. Perhaps he had been mistaken. No! He knew the town. He knew the street. It was the door—it didn't exist!

His heart beating hard, he walked quickly to the corner a third time. Without looking back, he turned the corner and walked faster and faster until he found himself running.

Staris opened the door to him and closed it quickly behind him.

"Feirek! Where have you been? We were afraid for you. Have you heard the news? Every street and wynd is smoldering with it! What's happened to you?"

Feirek could only shake his head and return Arela's warm hug with a clinging embrace. Others gathered around them.

"Something happened yesterday evening near the street of the blind potter," Toseny said. "We don't know what. We've heard a hundred different tales! You'd better sit down."

"This we know is true." Staris again. "Sirdde's viper is dead. Loughat was found lying across the lady's doorway with his own dagger in his back. That and these other tales have brought fire to the hearts of everyone. At dawn

Blygen's guards were sent through the streets, but not all returned. Three of the most vicious were found dead in the center of the tower street, not half a mile below the castle. It's said others found their way into the river. Now none dare ride alone."

"Then it's started already!" Feirek murmured.

"What's started? What do you know of it? Have you heard about yesterday evening?" Arela's words piled one atop another. "The hundred stories we've heard all have in common a boy and his sister near the street of the blind potter. You were on your way to Worul's rag shop. Was it Keld and Elylden? Do you know? Are they all right?"

"Give me another minute," Feirek begged. "I don't know where to start. Yes, it had to do with them. I . . . Give me something to drink."

He let go of Arela, sank into the chair, rubbed his hand across his forehead, and mumbled, "At least part of it's so, if others are telling it. Yes, I saw them. I know what happened. A fight . . . After that—ah, thanks, Arela—I thought I was going mad! I'll tell you of it and see if you think I have!"

It was some time after he had finished that Toseny ventured, "Do you think it was a dream?"

"No." Feirek shook his head. He pitied Toseny. The cut across the young scribe's face reached from temple to chin and would leave a bad scar. At least it had missed his eye.

Toseny sighed. "All that I wrote—lost in the river

when your boat tipped over. I've tried to write again but I can scarcely remember half they told us! Now this, and I have no more ink!"

"They must have ten times as much to tell as we heard," Staris murmured.

"What I wanted to ask him—the Wizard said good-bye for himself, but Keld and Elylden—from what he said, they'll leave here. Will we see them again? I pledged myself to serve that boy with the ring. I'll hunt for him and his sister to the end of the earth!"

There was a tapping at the door. It was Karos, as breathless as Feirek had been.

"Blygen's guards—they're setting fires. The poorest parts—the street of the blind potter is in flames from one end to the other!"

27

e looked at them thoughtfully. "You've a need of bathing."

Keld flushed. "There's been no chance."

"Here are soap and water. There is a basin. Do what you can. Your hair as well. It has a murky look." The Wizard frowned.

They did what they could, but Stilthorn was not yet satisfied. "Such rags are not seemly. There is a shop across the way."

He threw open the door. A smell of smoke was in the air, not unusual, though stronger than normal.

The tailor was pleased. A miracle he had clothes that fit as if they had been measured for them! Made for the leering old rake. "For a dear friend's children," he had said, and then his servant returned them—not even unfolded! A flaw in the style, he'd said, and not paid for them. Oh, everyone knew the gossip! The lady had turned him down.

He had cut and stitched so carefully, the cloth was so fine, so dear . . . He had cried last night. How would he pay for the cloth?

This man he had never seen—such dark eyes! Black! The granddaughter's the same. No back to them. They went on forever!

Why were his knees shaking, his hands trembling, and his heart beating so fast? The tailor sat down. What was wrong with dark eyes? A doting grandfather, whatever the color of his eyes and especially one with a full purse, was the best of all possible men in any country!

"We need a pair of horses." The grandfather turned back to him.

The tailor bounced to his feet, stretched his mouth into a teeth-gritting smile, and gave directions—did more. He saw them on their way, even made sure they had turned the corner before he returned to collapse once more at his bench. His wife came in a minute later to find him sobbing as she had never heard him do.

"Why, love, what is it?" she cried. "Have we been robbed?"

"N-n-no," he quavered. "He p-paid in gold!"

When he found animals that pleased him, Stilthorn told Elylden, "You'll ride behind me. There may be times we must run faster than the best pony can do."

That she would ride behind her grandfather made up for some of her disappointment in not having her own mount.

"Thosstoe, can he run fast?" Stilthorn asked.

"Fast enough!"

"Ah? All right then. A fine animal. We'd not want him to tire." He stroked the dog's head, mounted the horse. Elylden sat behind him.

"Hold around my waist, Elylden. We would not lose you."

The last trace of disappointment melted away.

Keld was already seated on his palfrey. They moved into the street. The Wizard looked over his shoulder. "Come. Ride beside me, Keld, as is befitting your station in this world."

The boy urged his horse ahead.

His eyes popping, the stable boy watched until they turned a corner. The horses were finer than he'd known! How they stepped!

Folk pressed back into doorways in the narrow streets, then peered after them. In the wider streets, people stepped aside and also turned to stare. Who were the silent strangers who rode with the bearing of kings, who passed so leisurely, so unafraid, through Adnor?

Two ragged urchins ran through the twisting ways to burst into a shelter of sticks and mud and cry, "He's found a way!"

Outside the door of a corner pothouse, Scroot picked himself up and dusted off his breeks. The drink had been worth the indignity. He blinked.

"Fruit of the vine preserve me, for the waters of Adnor never will!" He made a sign to fend off all spirits. "It's the boy with the ring, and his little wish-maid of a sister!" He blinked once more and shook his head. The vision did not disappear until it had rounded a corner.

His muttering was not lost on himself, for several standing nearby heard him.

"The boy with the ring!"

Heads turned even more quickly.

"The boy with the ring!"

Scroot wiped a trembling hand over his lips. "I said I'd tell her if I saw 'em again. She'd have the boy and I'd have the girl. But I'll never tell no lady of this! No thirst nor spots on the dice is worth standing twice afore *her*. And who was *that* with them?" His legs gave out from under him. Once more he sat in the street.

For whatever reason, no one tried to stop the three riders, not even a group of Blygen's guards who may or may not have heard the murmuring in the wide street of the tower. There was no need to harass travelers passing through the town when they had trouble enough of their own, for as the west wind quickened, smoke blew over and through the eastern streets of Adnor. A burst of flames rose suddenly and with it a black cloud tinged red. Was more burning than the street of thieves and rag-pickers? Had new orders been given? The guards turned their backs on the strangers and rode toward the castle.

The trio, a huge dog running easily beside them, passed under the gate and crossed the bridge with no question asked.

What need was there to challenge strangers on their leaving of the town? None thought to send word of them to the Lord Blygen or his lady. What need for the bother of small gossip?

The travelers took the road to the west.

"How will we draw her away? Where can we take her and keep her so Adnor will be free of her?" Keld broke the silence.

"We'll travel to the end of Blygen's domain and beyond," Stilthorn said. "There we'll try fishing."

"And Eddris is the fish?" Elylden asked.

"Perhaps. But we need one thing more than fishermen and fish."

"We need bait," Keld said.

The Wizard nodded. "Have you ever thought how bait might feel? No? Then learn now."

"You mean we're fishermen and bait both?" Elylden asked.

"Perhaps."

"Why 'perhaps'?" she wanted to know.

"Eddris too is fishing."

"Then we're all three! Fishermen, bait, and fish!" Elylden frowned. "But she can't catch us if we're not in Adnor!"

"When she finds her pond empty she'll fish in other waters. We'll take care to know where she casts her line."

"But *she's* the fish," Elylden insisted, "and we'll catch her because I always know where fish swim."

"I don't doubt you'll know where this one swims," Stilthorn said and then asked Keld, "What are you thinking?"

"I'm thinking that if we're all fish, I'd rather not swim in the same pond with Eddris."

Suddenly the boy pulled up on the reins, stopping the horse. "I'm leaving them! I'm running away! They helped us! I'll go back!"

"There's nothing you can do there but lose your life."

"But my friends . . . !"

"You will serve later."

"How? They're in Adnor, not out . . . somewhere . . . !"

"Remember. We are bait."

"I'd rather be bait in water than in fire," Elylden said. "So much of Adnor is on fire."

Both sides of the street of the blind potter, that of thieves and rag-pickers, burned through the night. The people of the streets behind it deserted their shops and hovels. Fire was eating its way through them as well.

Seven more of Blygen's guards vanished in the same night. A river dock exploded in flame. Five boats used to extract toll from fishermen were sunk.

The next day eight men were hanged and three children, a woman, and a blind beggar were ridden down in the streets by the dozens of guards who raged through the town. That night barricades appeared across alleyways. Bonfires leaped high at the corners of streets. The sky glowed red with other fires. In the morning, folk carrying bundles or pulling carts piled with their belongings began to appear on the bridge and fight to cross.

In the afternoon the Lord Blygen, surrounded by fifty of his guards, rode down from his castle. He rode through empty streets, passed shops with doors and windows locked and barricaded. Along the river he rode to the bridge.

"Tell them to fight their fires," he ordered and left twenty guards to turn back any who tried to cross, to turn them back into a rain of hot ashes, frantic pushing crowds, and smoke-filled squalor.

The Lord Blygen returned to his castle and called for his lady.

But the Lady Sirdde was gone. No one could tell him where.

28

"houldn't we go faster?"

"We'll not tire the horses, Elylden. We've a long ride ahead."

"Will she find us? How will she know where we're going?"

"Don't forget who she is. She will come to us at last."

"Because she's looked everywhere else?"

"Perhaps."

"Why didn't she stay what she was, instead of causing all this trouble?" Elylden grumbled.

"I don't know."

"Maybe she has opposites in her. Why do people have them?"

"People live between the Valley of the Nedoman and that of Fel."

Like Anna, he explained no more. She would watch for what he meant. Opposites. Did Anna have them? Did Stilthorn have them? Even with her arms around him she could discover nothing about him.

But Keld! "Why are you always fighting with your-self?" she asked.

"I'm not fighting with anyone. I'm thinking."

"It feels like fighting."

"Be glad I'm not fighting with you! How do you know anyway?"

Elylden smiled. She'd made him scowl even more! She hadn't teased him for so long! Her arms around Stilthorn's waist, she was happy.

A sudden peculiar feeling ran under her tongue, through her lower lip, up the side of her face, and settled between her eyebrows. Her palms throbbed. She straightened her back. Stilthorn had tensed. *Pay attention to the smallest things!* A faint bitterness lingered in her mouth. Nothing more. Thosstoe trotted beside them. Keld fought with himself. Stilthorn was calm. She relaxed.

Why was Keld afraid to talk to him? No grandfather could be as wonderful! She rested her head against the Wizard's back, then sat straight again. What *was* it? She glanced at her brother. He hadn't felt it. He was looking at his hands. Why was he so unhappy?

Keld chewed his lip. This powerful, soft-spoken, terri-fying grandfather—what did he expect of him? *You are no wizard, Keld.*

He hunched his shoulders. *And the Knights of Ahln?* Heat rose to his face. How had he dared say he would tell the Knights of Ahln how they should fight! His stories of them to Nichil, Parso . . . He hadn't thought to tell his new friends good-bye! His shoulders drooped. How could he fight with a sword when he had never held one? When the Wizard pushed aside his cape to mount the horse, he'd seen the sword *he* wore. Short, the hilt decorated with a gold band and black stone—seeing it had made his hands feel odd, his stomach tighten.

Could he prove himself? Kill a man? He rubbed his arm that ached, burned, and itched from the wound. His anger rose. Why hadn't he killed Loughat? If he ever saw him again, he would!

At evening they stopped at an inn. Elylden watched a stout peddler. No opposites in him! He was all growling stomach and eager hunger for beef and ale. Was this being one with the Wizards? But the innkeeper—though he smiled and smiled at a party of noisy guests, his thoughts were anything but pleasant! She yawned.

They would share a room. "A real bed!" Elylden exclaimed. "I haven't had . . ." Suddenly the Wizard whirled toward her and Keld.

"Your ring! Give it to me! Elylden, your sheep— from Anna!"

Keld tugged at the ring. Elylden felt in her pocket.

"Quickly! Yes! Now, both of you, your thoughts! Something other than yourselves! A broken bootlace! A chipped pot! A gnawed bone! Anything trivial! Quickly! Wipe everything else from your mind, think only of that. See it! Feel it in your hands! Smell it! Don't question me! Do it! Now!"

The command was so urgent Keld had no time to think. His eyes had fallen to a worn place in the rug. He fixed them on it, a dark, frayed spot. Bared threads broken, the scuffed floor showing. A burn?

Suddenly a freezing pain ran up the back of his neck, spread through his head and across the top of it, over his face, and into his throat. So swift it lasted only an instant, yet so shattering it left him with knees buckling as he sucked in a rasping breath. A hand over his mouth stifled his cry. He was pulled to a chair. The hand moved across his cheek and pressed the side of his face.

Keld half-opened his eyes to see Elylden kneeling, leaning against him, her eyes closed, a tiny whimper coming from her with each short breath she drew, Stilthorn brushing back her hair, his hand covering her forehead.

"Shhh. Hush. Sleep, both of you."

On their way early in the morning, Elylden said, "This road goes north. You said we would go west."

"We will visit the Fane of Monancien to see if Feirek speaks true and there is an opposite to what we've seen in Adnor."

She was quiet for a time, and then said, "I don't remember going to bed last night."

"You were tired. You fell asleep. I put you to bed."

Keld rubbed his forehead. Something . . . then Stilthorn's voice saying, "Sleep!" Nothing more. Had he been so tired too?

The fortress stood atop a hill and was surrounded by five thick earthen walls with a river running between the first two raths. The noon sun touched the sloping roofs of the great fane and its libraries.

"You will call me Zirawd here," Stilthorn told them.

"Or Grandfather?" Elylden asked.

"Or Grandfather."

A gentle Brother Quinolur took Keld and Elylden through blossoming summer gardens, pointed out the beauty of the spires, showed them tapestries, bronze statues, bowls and chalices of rare metals, all of elaborate and breathtaking art. In the libraries were manuscripts illuminated in brilliant blues and red, enhanced by gold leaf. They watched the scribes working carefully on exquisite parchments.

Overwhelmed, Keld murmured, "How can there be such a place outside the Valley of the Nedoman?"

"What do you know of the Valley of the Nedoman?" Brother Quinolur's eyes widened.

"What do *you* know of it?" Elylden asked him.

He laughed. "Only what is in a book we have."

Elylden admired a bronze figure of a man on a rearing horse. "I'm glad my grandfather decided to come here. Where is he?"

"Monancien asked Brother Graphuys to bring your grandfather to him."

Brother Graphuys pursed his lips. *What brought them here?* His eyes narrowed as the tall unknown bowed his head to Monancien.

Frail and slight, wrapped in a blanket of soft wool, Monancien sat before a fire. His face was as wrinkled as crumpled linen. His hands trembled. His voice wavered.

"By your eyes I see that you are a wise man. I wish I could discourse with you, but my wit isn't what it was. You came alone?"

"Zirawd brought his grandchildren. Brother Quinolur is showing them the fane." Brother Graphuys answered quickly for the stranger.

Brother Quinolur must watch those young people. If they had light fingers . . .

"Children? I never see them! Bring them to me, Brother Graphuys."

"You must not tire yourself."

"Just to look upon them."

"I think it better . . ."

"At once, Brother Graphuys."

"A young face delights an old heart. The weariness that comes with age is erased when their joy in living is . . ." The voice faded in Brother Graphuys's ears as he hastened away. What would Monancien talk of with this stranger? The affairs of the fane were best kept secret.

When he returned, Monancien and the stranger were talking of roses. There was an edge to Brother Graphuys's voice when he summoned the children from the hall.

"For only a moment," he warned stiffly.

"Good Brother Graphuys, fetch us a little something to eat and a drink. Don't worry. I shall nap soon."

Brother Graphuys bowed his head and muttering through tight lips, left the room. Monancien smiled, his wrinkles deepening. "Brother Graphuys is overly serious, but he is devoted to the temple."

Monancien liked to tease him! Elylden could not help grinning.

"Now come close to me. Let me hold your hands and look into your faces." Monancien took Elylden's hands, and peered into her eyes.

"My! Oh, my! A daughter of long ago! I see that you cry easily, because things don't happen as they should? Heed the words of your mother and your grandfather, my child. Curb your temper and most of all, do not mix what you imagine with what is. Mmmm. Your grandfather said nothing of this!"

Then he took Keld's hands and turned them over and back again.

"What's this?" He pointed to the ring and turned to the Wizard. "You've brought the son of the great-grandson of Benelf?"

Without waiting for an answer he spoke to the startled boy.

"We know of your father and learn at last of you! Your father died before you were born, hmm? You see, he followed Anna from Adnor to the Valley of Hune—so we assumed—for he loved her. I doubt he meant to desert his people. Doubtless he hoped to bring her back, for where else would he go that he vanished forever? So long ago. So very long ago. You knew that?"

Keld was speechless. The ring, the verse, Anna . . . his father . . .

"No? At last we know it's true, so now we understand more. When she knew she had to leave that place, he followed her again. How she must have pleaded with him to stay, for he was mortal. He could go into the valley, but he could not come from it and live long. So it would be for you, hmm? I advise you to stay from it. Do not even come near it. It is one thing for your sister, another for you. By all means, stay far from it's edge. We need you to restore what was lost to us when your father left.

"Now, these are my words to you both. Ignorance is the destroyer of the labors of man. Fear it. Next, fear greed. It takes what is necessary to others, and values those things that give no comfort to the taker." He leaned forward, as if imparting a secret. "Knowledge, now, though never satisfied, at least is comforting!

"Ignorance, greed, and arrogance, for arrogance . . . oh, hum, the list is endless. So many pitfalls! Your grandfather talks of them?

"Ah! Brother Graphuys is impatient. He thinks I am an old and garrulous creature. So I am. Go. Take your fruit and drink to that next room. Brother Quinolur is waiting." He gestured. "You too, Brother Graphuys. I will talk with their grandfather."

With no chance to say a word, they were dismissed.

"Now, Wizard, I have spoken to your grandchildren as well as I could. Was that why you brought them? What do *you* have to say to *me*?"

The shadow of a smile had crossed the lips of the Wizard. Now he grew serious. "They have seen man debased. I would have them see that he can also create rare beauty." He hesitated, then added, "Something has occurred that they do not remember. One day it may rise to their minds. Recalling your wisdom and the beauty here will comfort them.

"My words for you? If you value the splendor of your art, the poetry and histories that lie in your manuscripts, your tapestries, and your brotherhood, see that they are protected."

"Brother Graphuys says we are strong. Besides, how could any man destroy such treasures fashioned by his own kind?"

"You've lived too long away from the world. Knowledge and beauty challenge the tyrant's authority. There is insurrection in Adnor. Your fane lies within the domain of Blygen. That brutal lord would not be true to his kind if he did not suspect a temple devoted to thought! The learned are the first to be slaughtered, art the first to be destroyed. If you think not, you have a blind spot . . ."

"You don't have one?" Monancien interrupted. "Your grandson's is the blood of Anna and Stilthorn, but it is also the blood of Benelf."

"I know that he is very human."

"Think twice, Wizard! He is mortal! Benelf gave his life. Will you ask of your grandson . . . ?"

"I must ask of him what he can give. But I shall remember your words. I hope you will remember mine."

29

heir horses were waiting for them.

Elylden smiled at Brother Quinolur. "Please take this. It's all that I have except Thosstoe. He wouldn't stay if I gave him to you."

"I thank you. I see it is something you have loved greatly." Brother Quinolur examined the small object and put it carefully into his pocket. He lifted Elylden to the back of the horse.

"I thank you, Brother Graphuys, for your hospitality," the Wizard was saying. "A word of warning. Look to your defenses."

"Our walls are high."

"The force will be strong. Bring in the people from your fields and villages. Let them help defend the fane."

"You are worried about the fane and its treasures, but you would have me bring louts, ignoramuses—clods among such works of art? Their clumsiness would be as destructive as the forces of Blygen!"

"They would see the beauty. They would not hurl

gold chalices at the enemy. Give them swords! They are your people. Give them your protection and they will give you their loyalty."

"They can take shelter within the outer walls, if there is need."

"Do as you will. Farewell, Brother Graphuys."

They took the road southwesterly.

"Brother Graphuys thinks they're safe. Are they?" Keld asked.

"No."

"Shouldn't we have stayed and fought beside them?"

"No. There are enough who would be glad to fight for them. If Brother Graphuys's arrogance and pretention prevent him from asking them, that is his decision."

"He's not the only one there! We could persuade others!"

"We can't."

"Will Blygen destroy the fane? What will happen to the brothers?"

"I cannot speak for all of them."

Keld stopped his horse. "We have to help them! *You* can help!"

"I cannot. I did more than I should by coming here to warn them."

How could he speak so calmly? "Anna said there were things of beauty in the Valley of the Nedoman. Would you fight to protect them?"

"I would."

"Then why won't you help protect those in the Fane of Monancien?"

"It is not my battle."

"Then it's mine! If you won't help them, I will! Take Elylden with you. I'm going back to fight!"

"Go if you will, great-great-grandson of Benelf, but remember why we travel. If you return to the fane you will bring Eddris as well as Blygen down upon them. Not one stone will be left atop another, not one brother will be spared, and you will be to Eddris as the gazelle to the lion. If you are to spend yourself, make it worthy of the loss."

Eddris! A mixed feeling of helplessness and rage along with a sense of terrible injustice filled the boy. Why wouldn't the Wizard stop her? If she wielded *her* power, surely he could do some small thing! "Why couldn't you make Brother Graphuys change his mind?"

"Would you have your mind controlled by another? What use are the thoughts of others if they are no more than your own?"

His mind . . . He shuddered. Gooseflesh spread over him. He rubbed his forehead. What was it? A . . . nothing.

"Come with us, Keld." Elylden, her voice sober . . .

Us! Elylden and Stilthorn! I don't belong to them! My father—died. Elylden's father? What difference did it make who he was? She had Anna's power! My great-great—how many greats?—grandfather Benelf fought. He would fight again! Me—I'm running away! Adnor is burning. The great temple of Monancien will fall and its wonderful treasures will be lost while I ride off with a wizard and the daughter of a Woman of the Nedoman, without ever lifting a finger to help!

His role was to be bait. A bug. A worm.

Heartsick and sullen, Keld turned his horse around. He could meet the eyes of neither his sister nor his grandfather.

A gray-fingered cloud obscured distant fields. "Is it fog?"

The Wizard's answer was curt. "No. It's Blygen's smoke."

"From the fires of Adnor? That's too far away!"

"They've spread their damage."

The air thickened more until, from the top of a hillock, they looked on smoking fields of black ash, islands here and there still in flames.

"They've burned the harvest! What will people have for winter?"

"Nothing. But it doesn't matter."

Shocked, Keld looked at him. There was a set of the Wizard's mouth that made the boy hold his tongue.

They saw it soon, the burning hamlet, a cluster of half a dozen houses, the thatched roofs gone, the fallen timbers licked by flames.

If help was needed . . . They spurred the horses and in minutes were as close as they could come for the heat. There was no sign of anyone.

"Might they have run away?" Elylden asked in a small voice.

"No."

Even as the Wizard spoke, they heard a cry, half wail, half scream. A man ran toward them. He stumbled, fell, got to his feet, and came on. As he neared them, Stilthorn leaped from his horse, ran to him, seized, and held him.

A young man, his eyes wild, fought against the Wizard.

"Let me go! My wife! My son! My brothers! My father and mother! All of them! All of them! Let me go!" He struggled harder yet.

Keld slipped from his horse to help the Wizard. But suddenly the young man covered his face and began weeping. He slipped to his knees, his head bowed to the ground.

"The sheep!" he sobbed. "On the other side of the hill. I didn't know until I saw the smoke. My darling! My baby!"

Keld became aware that Elylden too was sobbing and wailing. Used as he was to her crying, this was different. She was choking, gasping, then wailing and screaming. Stilthorn lifted her down from the horse, shook her, and spoke to her roughly.

"Be quiet! Stop it! It won't do! It won't help!" He shook her again, making her head snap back and forth.

The screaming stopped, but she still sobbed. "It's bad!" she cried. "It's so bad! It's so bad!"

"Yes, it is!" Stilthorn said and shook her again, this

time more gently. She threw her arms around him and he held her close, stroking her head and murmuring to her.

It was not until then that Keld realized what else he was looking at—the slaughter that had taken place before the burning. At once he was sick, his stomach turning again and again.

"You'll find no blood to drink here, you murdering dogs!" the voice quavered. "For mine's dried to a black powder and will draw the sweat back through your skin till the salt shrivels the meat of your bones. There's naught but strings on my bones. Chew on them if you will, but they'll stick in your craw and choke you dead!"

The cottage door Stilthorn had swung open revealed a crone, old and withered, but with fiery eyes of hatred glaring from her face. She was the only person left in the next village they had come to.

"We've not come to kill but to ask your help," the Wizard said.

"I'll give no help to Blygen's brutes."

"We're none of Blygen's. Derin, the shepherd, needs comfort."

"You'll not find it here. Go to Glawth castle. The Lord of Glawth is no spring lamb, but they run to him to be out of Blygen's claws."

"Will you come with us?"

"No. I'll stay to curse Blygen to his face."

30

'll hang the man who sheds a tear for Blygen!" roared the fierce Lord of Glawth Castle, and he struck the board so hard the mugs rattled to the end of it. "They say his bride of little more than a month—the Lady Sirdde—has left him too."

"Has she."

"She's beautiful. No mistaking it."

"She's come here then? You've seen her?"

"No. Only the word of others who've seen her riding through the land. But I'd welcome her. I've a taste for beauty." He grinned and showed such pointed teeth Keld was glad he was no enemy of theirs.

"So, little mistress of the big eyes. Why do you look at me that way?" the Lord of Glawth said to Elylden.

"They also say . . . she's a wicked lady," Elylden told him.

"Why, I've heard that too." He struck the board again and laughed loud. "Which doubles why I'd like to meet her! For I've a fondness for wicked ladies. What do you say to that, little mistress?"

Holding his breath, Keld waited for his sister's answer.

"They say . . ." Elylden hesitated. "They say she's *very* wicked. I would be afraid of her."

The Lord of Glawth roared with delight. "There'll never be a woman I fear! I hope she comes this way!"

Stilthorn said, "She may. I only hope you're disappointed. Thank you for your hospitality, my Lord of Glawth. We must be getting on."

The castle of Glawth well behind them, Keld asked, "Why did you say that, Elyl?"

"Somebody had to warn him."

He looked at her quickly. Elylden—for all her prattle . . . And it was there again! Keld chewed his lip. Twice before he had caught that look on her face, a startled anxious look, as if she suddenly knew some frightening thing. No more than a flicker, it passed quickly, not staying the way it had when she huddled on the street in Adnor.

Sirdde—Eddris, this shadowed woman . . . *We will draw her away* . . . He wished the Lord of Glawth had not talked of her. The farther they were from Adnor, the stronger he felt her presence.

"We're out of Blygen's domain, aren't we? Where are we going now?" Elylden asked the Wizard.

"To a place I know."

"How can you? This isn't your world!"

"It was once."

"Does—someone know where we are?"

"Not yet."

"She's still looking for a pond with fish?"

"She is." Stilthorn half-turned to her. "Do you know of one?"

"No." She frowned.

A smile on his face, Stilthorn's eye caught Keld's. "You have a most persistent sister!"

"I know!" A smile came to the boy's face and with it a warmth toward his grandfather he had not felt before. It drove away the chill of Elylden's question. This—being bait, never knowing . . .

Elylden began once more. "Tell me about Anna. What do the Women of the Nedoman know? How do they know? Where did they learn it? How do they use it?" And one day as they sat in a small wood before a pile of twigs, "Why don't they use it differently?"

Stilthorn laughed. "How, differently? I don't know! I'm not a Woman of the Nedoman. I'm only a Wizard!"

"They could come here to help us. *You're* here!"

"No, they couldn't. And I am here for only one reason." Then abruptly, "Let me show you how to bring fire from your fingers. A gift from your father."

"My *father*?"

"All of your mind must turn to it. Watch! Hold your hands so . . ."

"But . . ."

"You had a father too."

"But Anna is the one . . ."

"Come! Let me see you bring fire to these sticks. We would warm our hands at it!"

"You have flint and steel! It'll take me a long time to learn!"

He waited.

"I suppose you have your reasons." If Elylden grumbled more, she did it silently, for Stilthorn was deaf to complaints.

Keld watched the lesson. Why would the Wizard answer one question and not the next? Where must they lead Eddris? When she came . . . His stomach knotted.

They had climbed well into the mountains now.

One night Elylden woke, sobbing. "They're burning the fane! Brother Quinolur . . . I don't know if my sheep is helping him!"

"Your sheep?"

"I gave it to him."

"Oh, Elylden!"

"Why shouldn't I? He was kind! He loved everything so much! I loved him. Was it wrong?"

"No, no. It was to be."

Keld ground his teeth. With all of Stilthorn's power, his knowledge, his wisdom . . .

The next morning Stilthorn seemed tired and preferred not to talk. Keld kept silent and mulled over what they had spoken of the day before. Games of skill. The Knights of Ahln proved themselves in them.

He had been put off when Stilthorn said, "They are

good only if the winner has no disdain for the loser, and the loser has no envy." He had looked keenly at Keld. "It's not wrong to compete or to win! It is how it's done. The best thing wrongly used can become the worst. Disdain and jealousy are worms for hatred.

"Look at Thosstoe! He vies with no other dog, yet he runs the best he can. Even sideways! His pleasure comes from that, not from knowing he does it better than every other dog in the world!" He had smiled. "I admit, he doesn't have to weigh the value of what he does. I don't want you to think you are Thosstoe."

Keld had laughed. Thosstoe had no questions. He loped beside the horses, was glad for a meal, a hug and a combing from Elylden, and a place to stretch out at night.

The nights grew colder, the days shorter, the climb steeper. Each place they stopped where there was no inn, no house to share, the Wizard left behind a small cache of food.

"For other travelers," he said.

They came to a cottage. A grizzled shepherd welcomed them.

"Why into the mountains?" he asked Stilthorn. "There's no more folk above me, and nothing ahead but winter."

"We've a place to go," Stilthorn answered.

"Snow often comes early. It's no time to take your grandchildren."

"I thank you for your concern."

"Do you know what lies there, man? It's no *place* to take your grandchildren!"

"I doubly thank you. When they come back this way, I hope you will welcome them once more."

"I'll do that. And you too."

Stilthorn nodded once, and they talked of other things.

The next morning, for the first time, Stilthorn answered a question before it was asked.

"We have a meeting in these mountains."

"Is she waiting for us?" It was Keld who asked.

"No. But she will come."

3¹

lylden gathered twigs and sticks.

"Well?" Stilthorn asked.

Keld too waited for her to hold her hand over the kindling.

"I can do it another way." Her hands in her lap, she bent closer, her eyes intent on the wood. A curl of smoke rose, a flame leaped up.

"Well done, daughter of . . . Ericoth," Stilthorn murmured.

That night Keld dreamed he was trying to run. As if chains bound him, he could not move. He struggled and fought until he woke.

Stilthorn stood before the fire, his head bowed, his arms at his sides. The night was breathless. Then his cape stirred as if by a breeze. The Wizard raised his head. A coldness touched the back of Keld's neck, and in the same instant a single flame leaped from the fire as high as the treetops.

The boy gasped, and started up. Only a shadow fell

between him and the fire! No, his eyes had tricked him. The Wizard was here, silent, his arms at his sides, his head bowed once more.

Keld sank back. The sense of another coldness came to him, a coldness he had forgotten. It had started the same way—at the back of his neck—he was looking at . . . then like ice, freezing . . . to take from him the sight . . . wiped from his mind as if he had never seen . . . It was at the inn before they went to the fane where he had seen the beautiful bowl etched with the words *Would you have your mind controlled by another?* No! Not words. They were figures, graceful . . . He clung to the memory of the dancing figures until he slept.

They came to a deserted hut set above a mountain lake, the frozen water dusted with snow. The sky of salmon-pink clouds showed through leafless birch and poplar that bent and straightened in the wind. Dark pine, the tops tinged orange, reached to the pale blue above them. A thin new snow scantily covered the fallen russet leaves. They watched the light change, the sky edge with lavender, darken.

"So beautiful, this world," Stilthorn murmured. "To destroy it . . ." He shook his head.

Who would destroy it, Keld wondered as he and Elylden scooped snow to melt in an ancient iron kettle. Stilthorn kindled a fire. He laughed shortly as a draft of chimney air blew smoke into the room, stinging their eyes and making them cough.

"I don't think it's funny," Elylden protested, wiping away tears.

"Nor do I," said the Wizard.

"Why did you laugh?"

"We'll need more snow than that," was his reply, and Elylden went muttering to fetch more.

The simple meal finished, they sat before the fire. Keld recalled a night when he and Elylden and Anna . . . His eyes met his sister's.

"Anna?" she said suddenly, a question in her voice.

"What of her?" Stilthorn asked.

"Sometimes I want her so much," she said. "I need her!" She put her head down on the Wizard's knee.

Stilthorn stroked her hair. "Remember all you can of her tonight. Remember what I have told you of her when she was a child. Think of her as she is now—forming the golden band of her power from what she learns as she studies the books of the knowledge of the Women of the Nedoman." He paused, then added, "Those that were written by her mother."

Elylden looked into the flames and thought of Anna. Keld too began to think of her when his mind made a sudden leap. Anna's mother! She had been Stilthorn's wife! He had been married, his grandfather, this Wizard, to Anna's mother, to his and Elylden's grandmother! Of course he had known that, but he had never *thought* about it! Anna's words, *I don't remember my mother.*

"Where . . . ?" he began.

"She is dead," the Wizard said shortly.

She had died? A Woman of the Nedoman? But what . . . ? How . . . ?

"Wh-was she . . . beautiful, your . . . Anna's mother?"

"Yes, she was beautiful. She was everything." His hand grew still on Elylden's head.

Keld's mind spun.

Stilthorn's voice broke the spiral of his unasked questions.

"Tonight I have something to tell you."

This night is like the last night with Anna—the night when everything changed! Keld didn't want to hear what Stilthorn would say, but there was no shutting out his voice, quiet though it was.

"Tonight the shield of my power has come to an end. We must talk of Eddris."

ill she come here? To this house? Tonight?" Elylden asked.

"No. I've led her astray. It will take her some
days yet. We'll go on, but she knows the way we have
taken. We must be ready to meet her."

"Where?" Keld asked.

"Beyond these mountains lies the Valley of Hune."

Keld was numbed. "Are you . . . are you taking us
there?"

"No. I would never do that. I only hope to be near it."

"Will your power be greater then?" Elylden asked.

"Yes."

"We could have ridden faster!"

"No. The time with you has been most precious. We'll
come close enough."

"You'll leave us then," Keld said slowly.

"Yes."

"No! We'll go with you, wherever you go!" Elylden cried.

"Your place is here where Anna sent you. You and Keld together."

"And Sirdde—if she doesn't return to Adnor, where will she go? What will she do?" Keld asked.

It was a moment before Stilthorn answered. "I don't know."

The boy grew cold. Her power must be great if she could find them after the Wizard had sent her elsewhere! Was it greater than that of Stilthorn? He grew colder yet. Who was there to help them? Might the Knights of Ahln come? No. Anna said he would not see them. He looked at his hands.

"If you were to go on and take Elylden with you because the Valley of Hune is for . . . I don't have the power of . . . If I were to go another way because . . . You said if I went to the Fane of Monancien she would . . ."

"Think a minute," Stilthorn said quietly. "I would hear you say it clearly."

Keld swallowed and tried to bring his stumbling thoughts together.

"If we went separate ways and she followed me and found me . . ."—he bit his lip, then burst out—"digging rocks from poor soil or milking a cow, why should she bother about me? But it might give you and Elylden time to come to the Valley of Hune. You would be safe there, wouldn't you? I can't go there. Monancien said I shouldn't."

He hunched his shoulders and frowned. He still was

not saying what he must. He looked into the Wizard's face. "Take Elylden. The gifts Anna gave her—there's nothing like them in this world! But I'm—common, ordinary! Hardly kin to what you are! What would it matter?"

Keld looked aside. He could not bear the probing gaze.

Again it was a moment before the Wizard answered. "Know that there is virtue in bringing poor soil to bloom and taking milk to a hungry child. Then answer me this, son of Anna. If your sister and I did what you ask, would we not be lower than common, and unworthy to be kin to the meanest of thieves?"

Keld flushed so hot his eyes stung. "I didn't think of it that way."

"I know. No more than I think you ordinary, great grandson of Benelf. We'll sleep tonight and travel tomorrow and the next day. And the next. When the time comes to face Eddris . . ." Keld's eyes were drawn back to the unfathomable look of the Wizard. "I would be pleased to have my grandson at my side."

"We'll ride as fast as the mountain wind!" Elylden cried as Stilthorn pulled her onto the horse.

Three days to that valley? How close must we be? Keld wondered.

They traveled swiftly the first day, and again the second, climbing high into the mountains. But the morning of the third, snow began to fall. By early afternoon it came so thick they could scarcely see the trees beside them. Stilthorn went slowly, but with no hesitation. Keld followed closely. Once the snow abated and they found themselves on a windswept rock, an island in a sea of lowering clouds.

"There's a cavern ahead of us, a place of rest," Stilthorn said. "If the clouds weren't so heavy we could see it from here."

The snow again whirled around them.

"Thosstoe!" Scarcely able to see the tips of her own boots, Elylden called the dog.

"He's with us," the Wizard assured her as he took the reins from Keld's hands. Head bowed he urged his horse on, leading Keld's.

They went even more slowly through the blinding whiteness but with no misstep and came at last under the shelter of a ledge of rock. Before them opened the wide mouth of a cave, a dark arch fringed with ice. Thosstoe shook snow from his back, the ripple of the movement carrying to the end of his tail with a flourish.

"How did you know it was here?" Elylden asked as they led the horses into the cave.

"I've been this way before."

Her mouth dropped open. *"Up from the Plain of Tregaed, through the Black Mountains, and into the Valley of Hune,"* she whispered. Then, "Are these the Black Mountains?"

"Yes."

"Did you stop here on your way? Here in this cave?"

"Yes."

"All of you?"

"Yes."

She looked with awe into the darkness. "The Knights of Ahln and the Wizards and the Women of the Nedoman! All of you! It must be big!"

"It is."

"We would never have found it ourselves, would we? Keld and I?"

"No."

"Is the path to the Valley of Hune over this mountain?"

"No."

They gathered sticks and pine needles to kindle a fire.

"There are logs piled against the wall where the horses are tethered. Bring some to me, Keld," said the Wizard as he blew gently on the glowing moss. He glanced toward Elylden who was watching him. "I know you can do it better. Feed the horses. There's hay near the entrance."

"Hay?"

"We are provided for. We provide for those who help us."

"Horses are more than help. They're our friends!"

"True. Feed them."

Keld, his arms filled with more logs, wondered why Elylden did not do as she was told. She stood looking at the Wizard, her pout more serious than he had ever seen it. Stilthorn rose from the now crackling fire to dust his hands and to find her staring at him. He returned her look with a gaze as somber.

"I should know you by now," Elylden said after a moment, "but I don't. Is that because you're a Wizard?"

"Yes."

"I had to know. I like you all the same, Stilthorn."

"And I like you, Elylden. Now go and . . ."

"Feed the horses. I'm going."

Thosstoe settled near the blaze and began pulling frozen clumps of snow from between the pads of his feet.

The boy sighed and put down the logs. "Elylden always knows exactly what she thinks without thinking about it. I wish everything came to me that way! I wish I always even knew what I was thinking *about*!"

"Elylden's knowing is part of Anna's gift to her," the Wizard said. "But do not think her gifts to you are any less worthy. 'To know' is one thing, 'to think,' another. Thought is what man has in common with the Wizards— to learn, to consider what you have learned." He paused and added abruptly, "She has need of knowing. You have need of seeing all sides of things and deciding. Respect both ways."

Suddenly Stilthorn smiled and shook his head. "Children of Anna! I have had to answer more questions in these few months than in all the time I've dwelt in the Valley of the Nedoman!"

"That isn't true," Elylden called.

"Perhaps I exaggerate," Stilthorn said, "but only a little."

They were comfortable near the blaze. Though the

glow of it reached far, Keld could see neither the roof nor the back of the cavern. The walls stretched invisible on either side of the entrance.

Elylden explored as far as the light would take her. She found drifts of leaves piled near the mouth of the cave. "Enough for beds for us," she called and returned to the fire. "It goes farther than I can see. Could I ever find the end of it?"

"No. And don't try. You'd wander forever. Now, we've a storm to wait out. It will be a long night, twice that of the day. How shall we amuse ourselves? Did you have games you played on winter evenings?"

"Anna would sing to us," Keld said. "Or tell us stories."

"Or we would have riddles, or make our own rhymes," Elylden said.

"Or play chess," Keld went on.

"If I had known that, I would have played with you." Stilthorn smiled.

Keld could not imagine what chance he might have in playing against a wizard when only once had he won against Anna! He laughed aloud.

Elylden frowned. "I don't want to be amused tonight."

"What then?" Stilthorn asked.

"You brought me Pareth's sheep from Anna," she said slowly. "You brought me something else too. When are you going to give it to me?"

It was the first time Keld had seen the Wizard taken aback. He looked long at Elylden before he murmured,

"You are indeed Anna's daughter, but you are too young for this!"

"And you are a wizard, but what you have doesn't belong to you."

Again Stilthorn was startled.

"Elylden!" Keld warned.

"No, let her speak," Stilthorn said.

"I kept Keld's ring for him. I can keep what you have."

"What I have is not Keld's ring."

"I know. But having it is making you tired. You must give it to me tonight. I can hide it. I can keep it safe."

"Hide it? Find a place, perhaps, but never to hold, never to keep."

Elylden's look did not waver before the Wizard's. "What did Anna say?" she asked suddenly.

"She didn't say. I told her to give it to me, and she did."

"Then I shall have to find out by myself what to do with it," Elylden said. "She told me I'd know when the time came. I've always known what I needed to know. Except once. That was the day in the street when Sirdde was in the carriage. It was all too fast for me. But I've known you had something for a long time. When I put my arms around you, I felt it here." She touched her underlip. "It's very strong. Will you show it to me? Please? So I have time to learn."

"You won't touch it!"

"I won't."

Stilthorn nodded, loosed his cape, and removed the shoulder belt that crossed his chest. Turning it down on the ground, he unfastened a lacing on the inside of it and drew out an object.

He held his hand toward the fire, palm up, fingers outstretched, that both Elylden and Keld could see what lay in it.

It was a band of gold, a perfect circle somewhat larger than his palm and plain of any design or inscription.

"This is the golden band of Eddris," he said, "the perfectly wrought symbol of her knowledge and power. A thing of great beauty."

Keld was transfixed. A narrow gleaming circlet—it was indeed beautiful. He looked from Elylden to the Wizard.

Elylden was scowling. She did not seem to be enchanted as he was by the perfection, the purity, the simplicity. Nor was the Wizard taken by it. Stilthorn had a look of puzzlement on his face.

"What flaw in her turned her from this, the spirit of the Nedoman?" he murmured. "How can she have wrought so perfect a thing and be so full of malice? How can none of that show here in the sign of her power?"

Elylden's face cleared. "It's because *you're* holding it!" she exclaimed. "Put it down. Let it be itself. I'll not touch it. I promise. Keld won't touch it. You won't, will you?"

Keld suddenly longed to hold it. What would it be to have such a piece of radiance in his hand! He curled his fingers tightly, the nails biting into his palms and shook his head, no. The Wizard nodded and gently placed the gleaming circle on the ground.

The golden band quivered. Keld grew dizzy. He put his hands to his head. The circlet twisted and turned, distorting in shape, changing in size, now smaller, now larger. Nor was it a simple band. It was a circle of writhing snakes, of tusked boars, of fearsome lizard-like creatures, of sea monsters, one devouring another. Eyes flashed red, shifted, or disappeared as it changed. Now it turned into human figures, distorted, misshapen, twisting in an agonized dance. They grew, were magnified so that the boy could see each contortion, every tortured grimace as the grotesque band buckled and racked them.

Like the cut of a knife, pain went across Keld's eyes.

"Enough!" the Wizard cried and reached out to cover the circlet. But Elylden was even quicker. Her hand was first and his covered hers.

As he leaped to his feet Keld heard Elylden cry out. Knowing that he was going to be sick and that Stilthorn would be far more able than he to look after his sister, he stumbled to the entrance of the cave.

When the retching stopped, he wiped his face and washed his mouth with snow. Ashamed, wet with sweat, cold and trembling, wanting desperately to lie down, he returned to the cave and the fire.

Elylden leaned against the Wizard, her eyes closed. Nothing was said. The golden band had vanished.

eld woke to find himself wrapped in a blanket and bedded in a thick layer of leaves. Warm, comfortable, he had no desire to move.

Swathed in blankets, Elylden sat up. "Are you feeling better?"

"Yes."

"Stilthorn said Anna gave you too much of something good or you wouldn't have been so sick. We have to stay here. The storm is worse."

He became aware of the sound, the wind moaning across the mouth of the cave.

"Where is Stilthorn?"

"Somewhere. He built the fire up and took a lamp and Thosstoe. He said I had to stay here with you. I have to feed the horses."

Keld lay back. He didn't want to know what good thing Anna had given him too much of. He didn't want to think about the storm or the wind or the horses or Thosstoe or even Elylden or the Wizard. He wanted to be warm and comfortable and to sleep and sleep and not to dream.

Elylden listened to the even breathing of her brother's sleep. If she could sleep it would help her forget. The memory was still sharp of Stilthorn instantly snatching her hand away, turning it over and pressing his palm against hers and clasping both of his hands tightly around it. Still, a terrible burning spread through her, a grinding, twisting sense of her bones being wrung by relentless strangling coils. But only for a second. The Wizard held her close and, though scarcely breathing, limp, and unable to move, she was then without pain.

She knew he eased her to the floor. She saw him go to Keld where he lay on the ground, wrap him in his long wizard's cape and carry him to the bed of leaves against the wall. Thosstoe came from somewhere to lie down next to him. Good Thosstoe, she thought, take care of my brother.

Stilthorn had picked her up and carried her deeper and deeper into the cavern until she became aware of a gentle light, warmth, a stone basin, and water. A cup to her lips. Time. Then he had brought her back.

"I didn't mean to touch it," she whispered to him as he settled her next to her brother. "I had to keep Keld from looking at it."

Keld heard the wind blowing. He heard Elylden rustling in the leaves and wished she would be quiet. He thought he heard her voice. He heard the Wizard say, "Let him sleep," and the boy was grateful to him.

It was dark when he woke the third time. There was none of the morning light that filtered into the cavern when he had wakened the first time, nor was there any sound of wind. Was he alone?

He sat up. At once his eyes were riveted upon the circle of red embers. An occasional blue-and-orange flame wavered from them. Now he heard Elylden's light breathing. Stilthorn? The glow from the embers was too faint to let him see. It must be night again.

Wide-awake now, he pulled and pushed away the heavy blanket. He brought a handful of leaves to the coals and blew on them. In the sudden flare of light he found sticks nearby and added a few at a time, building the blaze until he could set a log to burn in it.

He still could not find Stilthorn within the circle of unquiet light. Had he left them that he might draw Eddris from them? No, for his rumpled blanket was Stilthorn's cape! Keld shook the leaves from the heavy garment and folded it. Where was the Wizard? What was the white glow at the side of the cave? He walked toward it slowly. It was the moon shining on drifted snow at the entrance to the cavern. There was no footprint. Here were the horses.

Relieved, he returned to the fire. What had Stilthorn and Elylden done while he slept, what had they talked of? Had Stilthorn returned the circlet to his shoulder strap?

Even thinking of the terrible golden band of Eddris made his stomach turn.

Keld bent to pick up another log when a gleam at the back of the cave caught his eye. It was a faint light, seeming not too far distant. Was it a lamp? Might it be Stilthorn?

Without giving it further thought he put the wood on the fire and began walking toward the light. He was so puzzled by it that it was some time before he realized he must have walked a long way. Perhaps he should go back. But on looking back he could see no sign of the fire, nor could he find a wall on either side of him. Only the light ahead of him glowed. There was no choice but to go toward it.

As he kept on, the brightness grew. Here his outstretched hand touched a wall. Here steps rose into the mountain. Down these came the shaft of light.

The boy hesitated. A shadow fell upon him.

"Keld?"

"Stilthorn? I'm sorry!"

The Wizard's hand was on his shoulder. "What for?"

"I shouldn't be here. It must be a place private to you. I saw the light. I would have gone back sooner, but I couldn't find my way."

"There is reason for you to be here. Come."

It was a small grotto they stepped into. A shelf of stone circled the lower part, two lamps set upon it. Keld glanced at the Wizard.

"See," Stilthorn turned him half around.

Keld's lips parted. Before him was the statue of a young woman. She was seated, one arm around a small child who stood at her side. The other arm stretched forward, the hand turned up. In it lay a circlet of polished stone gleaming as one of gold might.

Keld knew he would never see anything more lovely. The curve of her body, the inclination of her head, the gesture of her outstretched arm—all were the work of such mastery the boy was left breathless. Beside that, her look was so full of life, so full of joy, he could scarcely believe she was not alive. He waited to hear her voice. And she was beautiful beyond words.

It was some moments before the Wizard said, "That is the likeness of Anna's mother. Your grandmother. That is Anna at her side. She was not quite two years old."

Keld could not take his eyes from the statue.

"The circlet in her hand is for her knowledge of healing, which she had completed. Though her knowledge of all things was vast, the smallest of bands was all she allowed herself. She would say, 'How can I say that I know? There are infinite questions! The ring will grow when there is nothing more to ask.' "

In some moments more he said, "Come. The night is almost gone."

Stilthorn took up one of the lamps and they left the room. Beyond the passage, the small circle of light showed no sign of cavern wall or marked way, but the Wizard did not hesitate. Keld walked beside him, and after a few minutes he found Thosstoe at his other side.

When they came back to the cavern Keld slowly added more wood to the fire. Over and over again Stilthorn's words echoed in his ears: *Yes, she was beautiful. She was everything.*

"You had better wake Elylden. The storm has passed. Eddris will be here soon. One word, Keld." The Wizard held up his hand. "At no time say anything of her golden band!"

Keld nodded, wondering if he would ever say any word at all for the rest of his life! He bent over Elylden and shook her. She sat up quickly, looked first toward the fire and then at her brother.

"She's coming, isn't she?" She wriggled out of her cocoon. "Are we still the bait?"

"The bait was taken a few days ago." The Wizard added still more wood to the fire, feeding it and feeding it so that the blaze widened and leaped as high and then higher than Keld was tall. Still he fed it. The light spread upward and outward. For the first time Keld could see to the roof of the cavern. Far above them gleamed a ceiling of icicles, inverted spires glittering with every color. To the sides it widened until the walls vanished. Behind them the cave stretched endless.

At last Stilthorn straightened.

"Are we the fish or the fishermen then?" Elylden asked.

"Keep adding wood, Elylden."

Elylden frowned as she put more wood into the fire.

"Keld?" To the boy's surprise, Stilthorn unfastened the belt from which hung the sword. He girt it around the boy, smiling slightly as he pulled the strap half around him again.

"I've . . . I've never used one. Wouldn't it be better for you to wear it?" Keld asked.

"It is not mine to wear. Now, your ring, let me see it." Keld moved to take it off.

"No, no. Just show me your hand. You wear it on the right. Good. You will carry the sword in the same hand. Draw it. When the moment comes . . ."

"I can't kill a woman!" Keld whispered, staring at the short blade and the hilt's ring of gold. There was a strange familiarity in the touch of it, the feel—as if his hand had held it before, a horse beneath him . . .

"I don't ask you to kill her. When she and I have had our words—you will know the moment—you will drive her from the cave, drive her up the mountain. Hold the sword before you, across your body—thus. Yes. She will not want to be touched by it. Force her back. Drive her, no matter what she does, what she says. Go toward her. Drive her! Do you understand?"

Keld nodded. His hand holding the sword was cold now.

"Your life, your sister's life depends upon you doing so! Elylden, come from behind the fire. Stay close to Keld. There—both of you, against the wall where you slept."

Suddenly the Wizard laughed. "I feel as I did when I was setting the stage for the performance of Darathyu's *Perdalis*. How long ago that was! Anna's mother was the leading lady. How she teased Darathyu for his passionate scenes! I suppose you've never been to a theater?"

Stilthorn spoke so lightly, Keld forgot why they waited.

"No," Elylden answered. "But Anna told us about them and we made our hands into puppets. Anna showed us how. What am I to do?"

"Of course she would have!

"*Think always of the fire, Elylden. Keep your eyes upon it. Do not let it go out.* And what stage did you have for your puppets?"

"A chair with a cloth draped over the back. What happened in *your* play?" Elylden asked.

"Why, as I said, your grandmother was the charming heroine, and Eddris . . ."

Suddenly he snatched up his cape. "On your knees!" he commanded pushing the startled pair against the wall and to the ground. "Keld! Hold her close! Don't speak! Don't move!" He threw his cape over them. Keld gasped at the weight of it, heavy as a shield of lead.

Even as the cape covered them, the cavern was filled with so blinding a light it came through the heavy cloth so that Keld saw Stilthorn whirl to face the entrance and throw his arms high, palms outward.

34

A wall of power, far stronger than that which had struck them on the river, rushed into the cave, damped out the fire, scattered embers across the floor, and left the cavern dark. Keld and Elylden, clinging to each other, were crushed back against the wall and held with a weight so intense they could not breathe.

Almost at once a spark of light came into the darkness. A thin flame of blue flickered and twisted in the center of the cave, and Keld could see again. His back to the fire, the Wizard stood facing the cavern's entrance. With the flame came a pulsing, a high singing. Then a flash of blue lightning rose from the narrow flame to the ceiling of ice and with it a crack of thunder that split the weight and shattered it.

Keld gasped. His ears rang. His head throbbed, but there was air for him again. Elylden sobbed once and then was still. He could feel the quick rise and fall of her chest as she, like him, fought silently to regain her breath. The cape seemed not so heavy, but something pressed against him with a different kind of weight. A vestige of the wall of power had not been driven from the cave.

Elylden moved slightly, turning from him toward the cave.

The blue flame continued to burn but neither as tall nor as bright. It hung above a small circle of fire that rekindled itself. Keld could not believe that only a moment ago its flames had leaped so high. Still, he could see by its light. The fabric of the cape seemed to have thinned.

The Wizard stood motionless, his arms low, hands out, with fingers spread. Darkness crept toward him from the entrance. The Wizard's arms moved forward. The darkness retreated. Again it came, rising higher this time, a cloak of blackness, filling the cave, cutting off the light of the flame as it approached him. Again it drew back.

The third time it came with a rush, a force of darkness like that wall of power, and with it a low vibration that made the air tremble. Again all light of the fire was swallowed up. The Wizard vanished. Keld could no longer feel Elylden against him. He knew only that his body was shriveling, his bones crumbling. He could see nothing, hear nothing. He was being absorbed into nothingness.

And then the blue light exploded, a thousand splinters of brilliance fracturing the darkness as the lightning had shattered the weight.

Feeling returned to him, the sense of his body, his arms,

his legs, of Elylden clinging to him. He could see once again, but a persistent low throbbing filled his ears, and, like the weight, a part of the darkness too remained. He felt Elylden grow even more tense.

The Wizard was now no more than a shadow. Behind him glowed a single low blue flame, pulsing, fading, casting almost no light. Beneath it lay flickering embers. The cloak against Keld's face had the lightness of fine silk. He was scarcely aware that it hung before his eyes. He tried to drive the weight from him with his mind, the half-darkness, the throbbing against his temples, but it would not go.

Minute after minute passed with only a stillness of waiting. The Wizard stood silent, his head bowed, his arms at his sides. The blue glow neither grew nor died. The circle of embers pulsed.

Then from the cave's mouth a mist crept in, cold gray trails of smoke turning and shifting like ghost serpents writhing across the floor, a thin layer of them spreading over it from side to side, hissing and twisting. It formed those shapes Keld had seen in the golden band, serpents, boars, vicious animals—and then the writhing agony of the figures of men and women, contorted, tortured, coiling. They began to grow in height. With fear Keld watched the rising, swelling forms. They will swallow us, and we will become a part of them, he thought suddenly.

The sinuously moving wraiths swirled around the Wizard's feet before he lifted his head.

"Eddris!" His low voice filled the cave.

All movement of the smoke-like eddies ceased. They hung just above the floor as if frozen. It seemed to Keld an eternity that they stayed, and then they began to thin. They twisted in upon themselves and slowly drew back. Suddenly all the mist drew back and vanished, and with them the weight was gone, the darkness was gone, the force was gone. The sound was gone.

The pale flame burned silently.

Into the silence came a single word to echo and re-echo through the cavern.

"Stilthorn!"

35

eld knew that the cape was still there only by the faint touch of gauze against his lips. Light of day came into the cave, the reflection of the sun shining upon the snow. A shadow was cast across the floor.

Stilthorn stood unmoving, his arms at his sides. Behind him burned a small circle of yellow fire.

The shadow on the floor slipped forward.

"Stilthorn!"

Though whispered, the name carried through the cavern as clearly as if it had been shouted. "Why are you here?"

"This place is sacred to me." The Wizard's voice, quiet as always, held also a tone of great weariness.

"But why at this time?" The voice, that of a woman, rose.

"I come as I will."

"I was not seeking you!"

Stilthorn said nothing.

"I came to destroy a power that would destroy the world!"

"Does Fel walk again?"

"No! A thing different from Fel! I thought it would be but a trifle, no stronger than that of flawed children. But I found one that does not belong here! An evil horror! Now I understand why the Knights of Ahln left the Valley of the Nedoman. I have risked my being to follow it! It passed through Adnor. Because of it the town lies in ashes. Hundreds have been slaughtered. Lord Blygen of the castle is dead. The Fane of Monancien has been burned, its treasures destroyed, the brothers slain. This terrible power fled from there! I followed it here!"

"You followed me."

"No! Not you! You would not have come through Adnor to visit this place! You would have come through the Valley of Hune. This power led me a hundred ways through this land before I came here! I would never have mistaken yours for an evil one!"

"There is no perfection in this world. You made a mistake."

A low moan filled the cave. It grew in a wailing crescendo that rose to a shriek.

"Why did you not call to me at once! I would have known you! Now I have destroyed your power! Stilthorn, I have destroyed your life!"

"Yes."

Elylden suddenly tried to pull away from Keld. He tightened his arm around her and slipped his hand across her mouth. "Think of fire!" he whispered against her ear. She grew still.

"But there is hope! You still live! Come with me, Stilthorn, to the Valley of Hune! It is not far!"

"No."

"You must! I will help you! You will be restored. I too need its balm, for in taking you for another I spent myself against you!"

"I know."

"We will return together to the Valley of the Nedoman. There we will regain all of our strength, our power, our knowledge, our perfection!"

"No."

"You must, Stilthorn!" the voice coaxed. "When we are strong again we will rule together in the Valley of the Nedoman!"

"I have no desire to rule, nor is there need for it in the Valley of the Nedoman—nor has there ever been such need among us."

"You are wise! You are powerful! You will be my mentor, the source of my knowledge!"

"The Women of the Nedoman and the Wizards and Knights of Ahln have always freely shared their knowledge—except for you, when you hid yourself away."

"To develop my golden band of the Nedoman! The most powerful that ever was! You are the greatest of the Wizards of Ahln, and I am . . ."

"The most vicious of sorceresses! You no longer deserve to bear the title of the Nedoman. The dishonor you have done to it is beyond speech, beyond thought."

"What knowledge do you have of me that you say

this? I am Eddris, the greatest of the Women of the Nedoman!"

"I am Stilthorn, father of Teyapherendana."

"But she is dead! She was unruly! She would not listen to me! She insisted upon leaving the valley! She died when she . . ."

"She did not leave it."

"Then you . . . ! Don't be a fool!" she cried suddenly. "Your power is gone! You are dying! A wizard's death is painful! One by one you will give up the names of your powers from the least to the greatest. Hard as you struggle against each loss, you cannot win. With each the pain will be greater. But the suffering will be nowhere near that which you must endure when you give up your knowledge, and then your life! I offer you life!

"Think of it, Stilthorn! You are already suffering! But this is nothing to what the last will be!"

"I know that."

"Then come with me! Why should you die? The greatest of the Wizards must not be such a fool!"

"You have done what you have done. Against all the laws of being you have crossed the boundary of the two worlds, brought your power here, used it where it should never have been used. Such action can only bring disaster to one, even destruction to both of these worlds. Why?"

There was a time of silence. Then came a whisper.

"I did not have what I wanted!"

"What could you want? Everything is in the Valley of

the Nedoman that anyone could desire! Love, peace, the joy of beauty, knowledge, the excitement of discovery! It was as much yours as anyone's!"

"It was not enough."

"Not enough! It is everything there is! Or would you bring what is here to it? Would you have us divided as men are? Capable on one side of the creation of what is sublime, and on the other of the most abominable brutality? What brought you to such corruption that you would think to destroy one of your own kind! From that deed a rot now creeps through the Valley of the Nedoman! It shatters our being, destroys our essence, the unity of life!"

"If you have been shattered it is by your own fault!"

"I speak of my daughter—trying to send her to her death. Now what will you do here that the all-knowing Knights of Ahln were drawn to man's world to protect it from you? What misery would you create in a place that has enough of its own? What possesses you?"

"What I wanted belonged to another. I was second! Always second!"

"There is no first, no second in the Valley of the Nedoman. We have always been one with each other and with all of life!"

"You are a fool! There is first everywhere! Now I will have what I want, for the others sleep—all but your Anna, and what does she know?"

"She is learning. What is it you want? Power?"

"The power, yes. The power is good. It helps. At first I thought it would bring me what I really wanted, but the longer the time passed, the more I feared I would never have it. Now I know I will never have that. But the power—I like it. I will keep it."

"The desire for power is an abomination. It is Fel!"

"Fel! Yes! When I saw Fel on the Plain of Tregaed I knew he was like you. The greatest of his kind! You have your opposite, Stilthorn!"

"In another world! What has brought you to this delusion?"

"When I saw him, I knew I could have everything that is not in the Valley of the Nedoman. He and I—we shall hold the power, he over his kind and I over mine. When we join, no wizard, no woman, no knight, no man— nothing—can stand against us!"

"To walk with him is to walk with death."

"Not for me! Death is for you, Stilthorn. I will not have a mortal as your daughter did. I will return now to the Valley of the Nedoman. There I will perfect the golden band of my knowledge—it is almost finished— such a band as has never been dreamed of in that valley! With it in my hand I will have no reason to fear that third power I sense to be so close. Not yours, Stilthorn! The other—the one I followed here. I want it! I will come back from that valley and join it to mine."

She was silent for a moment and then she laughed. "You don't answer me? You were great once, Wizard.

The greatest of them all. You will soon be only a man, as mortal as any. I would have something better. Fel is as great now as you were then."

"Go! Go quickly, Sirdde, before I walk upon your shadow." Stilthorn stepped forward. The shadow retreated. He moved forward again, and again the shadow retreated. Once more he would step forward, but he faltered, stumbled.

"You see? Already you are failing! How you will suffer! You should at least have saved enough of your power to return to the Valley of Hune! Where did you squander it? On some worthless mortal? But what is that to me? Yes, I shall go now. Let me pass."

"There is no one to stop your going, but you will not come this way. Go up the mountain, Eddris," he said quietly.

Keld heard the Wizard's words, and another command echoed in his mind. *Drive her up the mountain.* It was to him Stilthorn spoke.

The boy was shaking, his lips numb, his hands cold, his mouth dry. He struggled to his feet. The film of the cape dropped from around him as if it did not exist. Somehow he found himself at Stilthorn's side, took the Wizard's arm, and helped him to steady himself.

"Who is this?" the voice hissed.

"The son of Anna."

A sibilance like that of a pit of snakes filled the cave.

Keld, looking upon the bright snow, saw only a dark

form against the brilliance. Somehow he drew the sword. There was again an odd instant of familiarity, then a sharp throbbing in his hand as he grasped it firmly. The figure backed away, and the boy and the Wizard moved forward until they stood in the light at the mouth of the cavern.

"Look upon the face of Eddris. She was once beautiful," said the Wizard to the boy. "She was once a trusted friend, loved, as close as any sister. See how she still tries for beauty, still bears the guise of a Woman of the Nedoman. Then look behind those features into eyes of arrogance, upon a mouth thinned by cruelty, a face of deceit. Take no pity on those qualities! Have no mercy on them! But learn them, Keld, burn them into your memory so that whatever mask may be held up to hide them, you will forever recognize the true mien behind it."

Eddris replied to his words, her voice suddenly harsh. "Don't flatter yourself that you teach him, Wizard. I know with what small gifts your daughter indulged him. He is only human. Fallible, ignorant, powerless, he bears all the faults of his kind!"

"As did Benelf. But he knew good from evil."

"There will come a time, Stilthorn, when a grandson of Benelf will not know one from the other! When he calls the honest man a liar. When the scoundrel deceives with the face of innocence, when the fool is wise and the wise man is mistaken, when all things that seem are not so! In this time of deceit, beware for yours, Stilthorn! In that time my strength will be its greatest ever! The son of your daughter will be deceived! He will betray his kind!"

"Her son will ever remain true! Look upon the ring of Benelf, Eddris, and upon the sword that defeated Fel. And if those be lost, look upon the face! What lies there is enough for this world! Never will it show betrayal!"

Suddenly he leaned heavily upon Keld. "I can go no farther," he murmured to the boy. "You bear the sword and the ring. Use them now to drive this woman from our sight. As Benelf drew Fel, so you must drive her. Go, Keld. Drive her from us!"

"Stay or I will destroy you as I have destroyed Stilthorn!" she cried.

Stilthorn's quiet voice was at Keld's side. "Drive her from your sight."

The youth hesitated. Stilthorn—could he stand alone? Was he dying? Must he leave him? To carry this sword, the sword of Benelf—so short, yet how heavy it was! His head swam. To drive her away—would he be able to do it? Alone? How?

Suddenly the woman laughed. "He is afraid! Look, Stilthorn! Anna's son is afraid! What has she reared but a peasant boy!"

"A station in life is no measure of courage." As ever, his voice was quiet. "Go, Keld. You are needed for this. It is what you have waited for."

36

hat he had waited for? There was no horse beneath him! The sword he held was not to strike . . . There were no Knights of Ahln . . . *If I battled beside them, they would have to fight differently.*

His face suddenly hot, Keld let go the Wizard's arm and stepped from beneath the shelf of rock. He moved toward Eddris, following her onto the mountainside as she backed away.

"Drive her from you! Do not look back! Do not let her return in your footsteps!" Stilthorn's voice grew faint. "Be wary of her deceit! Stay from . . ."

Eddris' words came quickly to drown out his voice.

"So you will follow me, brave young man? Good! I will never leave your sight. I will walk before you forever!"

Keld could think of no word to say to her. Mouth dry, voice caught in his throat, he could only walk toward her. Though he strained to hear, no other word came from Stilthorn. Had Elylden come to his side?

★ ★ ★

Elylden wiped at the cobweb that brushed her face, then put both hands to her cheeks. It was no cobweb.

Carefully she gathered in the mesh of strands until she could feel no more drifting across her wrist. She closed her fingers over her palm. Then, one hand balled to a fist, she crawled to the dying fire. She found twigs scattered near it, gathered them, lay them on the embers, and blew on them until they flared. She found sticks and held them in the small blaze, one by one until they caught and burned, then crept to the wall of the cave and brought a small branch to the fire. Only when that too had begun to burn did she crawl to the mouth of the cave and Stilthorn.

On his knees, head bowed, hands before him in the snow, he did not answer to her touch. But when she uncurled her fingers and with the greatest of care opened and spread the faint gray gossamer over his shoulders, he drew in a breath.

"Thank you, Elylden," he whispered.

Holding to each other, they came to their feet.

Elylden found Thosstoe at her side. With one arm over the dog and the other around the Wizard, she turned from the entrance to the cavern.

"It needs more wood," Stilthorn murmured.

Leaving the dog at the Wizard's side, she brought logs and fed the fire until it burned high. Then the three started slowly toward the depths of the cavern.

It was easier to breathe and she didn't have to lean so

hard on Thosstoe. She couldn't help noticing that Stilthorn's step was firmer and that the cape now had the substance of silk. Deeper yet, the touch of velvet brushed her face.

They rested in the grotto.

"Can I take you all the way?" she asked.

"No. We'll stay here. I'm tired. Let me see your hands."

Wondering, Elylden held out both hands to him to examine.

"There's a spring, Elylden, just beyond the steps that come to the grotto. It fills a stone basin. There is a cup on the edge of it. Fill the cup. Hold the hand that covered the circlet to the ground. Pour the water over it. Don't let a drop fall back into the basin. Make certain the palm and all the fingers and your thumb as well are rinsed. Even your wrist. Fill the cup again and bring it to me."

The girl did as she was told.

He drank half the water and handed her the cup. "You must be thirsty too."

She was and, when she had finished that, thought she might even have more. But when she returned to the spring, no water flowed from the rock. The basin was empty and dry.

"We'll wait now," Stilthorn said when she came back. "Sleep, if you will." Suddenly he grew pale.

"What is it?"

"No matter. I'm tired."

She helped him lie down and folded her coat to put beneath his head, saying, "I don't need it. It's warm here."

"Yes," he said, then gave her one of his rare smiles. "I see as you always do, you have a question?"

"Yes. Two."

"One at a time then."

"Will Keld be able to drive Eddris away? She's so powerful!"

"Anna gave you each three gifts. The first was the same for both. You'll be aware of it when you are older. The second—" Stilthorn reached out and touched Elylden's hair. "Did Anna always cut it so short?"

"No. Arela did. But it's growing. It's not quite down to my shoulders. It used to be almost as long as Anna's, though I couldn't sit on it the way she could sit on hers."

"You look like your mother. Her second gift to you."

"But my hair is black, and so are my eyes. And my eyebrows too."

"The color of your hair or your eyes or your skin has nothing to do with beauty. You didn't see Sirdde's face as Keld does—the outward features of a Woman of the Nedoman, but unable to conceal the hideous distortion of what she is within.

"The third gift—the ring to Keld, and her words to you."

"But . . ."

"Eddris? If Keld can hold to Anna's second gift to him, he will forever drive off such evil."

Elylden sighed. This was the answer to her question, but like so many of Anna's, it was no answer for her. Maybe someday . . . Her brows came together.

"The second question?"

"Why couldn't you keep Eddris from us? You're such a great Wizard. And how could she be such a powerful sorceress and not know it was you? She thought she followed some terrible evil! Was she lying? Or did you deceive her? Or don't you know?"

"There's never a mystery in your questions, is there? Though I know you often find one in the answers you get." Stilthorn laughed, then grew serious. "She didn't lie. I kept her from us for a time, sending her elsewhere as she hunted. But the power of her golden band was stronger than I knew. I could not conceal it forever. It drew her to us at last."

"*That* was the evil power she followed?"

"Yes. I thought she would know it, demand it, take it. But consider, granddaughter of Stilthorn, she called it an unknown power. A third power. She admitted to fearing it. She believed her golden band to be still in the Valley of the Nedoman. Why? And this surprised me, Elylden. Her band is stronger than *she* knows. It has its own power that she did not recognize. If she had, daughter of Anna, we could not have stopped her from seizing what she herself had wrought."

Elylden wondered how Eddris could not know what she herself had made. "I suppose you have to think about that to understand it," she grumbled. "Keld is better at that than I am."

He had answered her second question. She understood enough about Eddris and the golden band. But it was little comfort. That "if" of Stilthorn's—*if* Keld can hold to Anna's second gift?

She was even more afraid for her brother.

37

rive me? No! Come with me! I am waiting for you!"

The pulse in his throat was hard and quick. He must fix his mind upon something other than fear! He must find a way to drive her!

What other way than to hold the sword before him, walk toward her?

Eddris backed slowly as he advanced, yet it seemed to him the ground rushed by beneath his feet.

"Fight me and I will bring grief to you forever," she cried suddenly.

He could answer only to himself. I will always fight you. Step by step he moved toward her.

"I will steal your children. I will maim you, cripple you, blind you, imprison you. I will drown you in the dark waters of my power. I will destroy the golden fruit of your trees. I will rule your thoughts. Then you will give yourself and your world to me!"

She continued to back away from him.

The sword grew heavier. Clamping his teeth together, he tried to reassure himself. Maimed, crippled, chained, imprisoned, blinded, I will fight you. I will never let you rule my thoughts. I will never give myself or my world to you.

For a time longer she continued to back away. Then she turned and climbed swiftly, over boulders, through snow and over windswept rock, higher and then higher, but never out of his sight. Keld followed. She fled up a narrow, twisting path. He followed. She was waiting for him. She vanished into a cleft in the rocks. He stopped. Was she gone? She appeared above him. He followed.

How far had they come? He dared not look back. The sword grew heavier yet. How he had wanted to carry one! How hard it was to hold!

Here they crossed a sheet of ice, there she clawed her way up a steep face of rock. She stopped to look down upon him and taunt him.

"I must wait for you at every step! How slow you are!"

Keld paused. He had to hold the sword with both hands.

"Your sister would not be so slow! She would have come quickly! She would not have feared me, she who has the gift of Anna's power."

What did she know of Elylden?

"Let me tell you about her, for I know more of her than you! Know this, grandson of Benelf! Her power is like mine. I understand it. As she watches the Wizard die, she feels her power growing and learns what her strength will be. Like myself there will be something she will always want. I understand that. I will find her. She and I will be of one mind. No wizard, no brother will stand between us!"

Elylden!

"Ah! I have touched you. You do not trust your all-knowing sister. How can you when you know nothing of her power, how she comes to know the thoughts of others! Come, come! Why must I wait for you!"

That she should try to make him mistrust Elylden! The same fury he had known when he threw Loughat's knife rushed over him. For an instant he wanted to do the same with the sword of Benelf. Throw it at her! Throw himself at her! Fight her! A mist came before his eyes.

He felt the touch of a hand upon his shoulder, heard the Wizard's voice. *Where are you going?* and again, *The fire of anger can blind you when you most need to see clearly.*

His fingers froze on the hilt of the sword. No, the Wizard was not at his side. It was only a remembered touch. He could not throw this sword as he had thrown a knife! To try would be to throw it away! He must not let her turn his thoughts her way! His anger dissolved. The air cleared as he had never seen it. Each crack in the rock, each twig of a bush, each flake of snow had meaning.

He must drive her.

Keeping her always in sight, he found a way around and up until he was face to face with her.

"How tired I am of waiting for you! I would really rather have your sister!" She frowned and murmured, "I saw her in the street in Adnor. I thought she was mine then, but she vanished. I don't know how. Just as the power of the ring came to me, and then vanished." Then her face smoothed. "But I have you now, and I will have her soon enough."

Keld shuddered before her cold smile. At last he found words to speak aloud. "You will never touch her!" He stepped toward her.

She stepped back. "What do you know of her?"

"She is my sister!" Again he moved forward.

"Only half."

"Our mother's blood." Another step.

"Your mother's blood is the same as mine! That of the Nedoman, and what good does it do *you*?" She walked on, then stopped and looked back at him. "I am waiting for you, little mortal. Do you drag your feet from fear of where I lead you?"

The sword was of such a weight his wrists ached. His arms to his shoulders ached, his fingers cramped. How much longer could he hold it? He started to follow, then stopped, appalled. I haven't been driving her, I've been following her! How am I to drive her? Where?

She was crossing and climbing a sloping shelf of rock. He could see only the sky beyond it. He stared up at her.

"Come along," she said. "Come here and stand beside me, grandson of Stilthorn. Look upon your world from a mountain peak! Look upon the world of the Great Wizard."

My world? His world? What world? Keld hesitated. How high had they come? *Drive her up the mountain!* Where were they? This tilted slab of rock—what lay beyond it?

Beyond these mountains lies the Valley of Hune.

"There are things you would do for your world, things Stilthorn would not do for you. Think of all that you would like to have, that you wish to do! Ah, how easy your face is to read! Listen to me! Let me tell you what you don't know!"

She was now at the very top of the ridge, her back against the sky. For a moment she was silent, then she cried, "Know that you can have his power! But if you are afraid to come and see what that is, you are not worthy of it! Come! Look!" She gestured. "You may choose then. You will come with me of your own will once you've seen these wonders."

The power to do what he wanted to do? Still he hesitated.

"Aren't you curious? I'm growing fond of you, silent one. Your arm is tired, isn't it? Rest here beside me and decide. If you choose my way, I'll return to fetch your sister. She will come when Stilthorn is gone and I tell her you are waiting for her. Then you will be together forever!"

Elylden! Would she go with Eddris to be with him?

Where would Eddris take her? What would she do
with her?

But how could he answer for Elylden? How for himself? Couldn't he think for himself? What did he want to
have? The world to be better—to be just! He knew what
that was! If he could rule so that everyone did as he
wanted them to do! To do battle beside the Knights of
Ahln! To defend . . . to slay all who opposed him! The
sword . . . No one would wrest it from him! Cheat him
of it . . .

He was shaking now, scarcely able to keep the point of
the sword from the ground. How could he climb this rock
and hold the sword before him? Eddris . . . offered . . .

What did he want?

She was calling to him. "Foolish boy! Come here! Tell
me you'll not stay beside me when you learn of what is in
your and your sister's blood. I will show you how you can
have the power that your sister has, son of Anna, kin of
Eddris!"

Son of Anna! *Would you have your mind controlled by
another?* Would he rule the thoughts of others? Eddris . . .
There was a touch of cold at the back of his neck and then
a sudden sharp vision of a tattered rug rose before him.
Dark, broken threads, a scuffed floor . . . the Wizard's
hand against the side of his face . . . and then, *What use are
the thoughts of others if they are no more than your own?*

Words he had forgotten! What was he thinking?

Not power, but thought! That was what he had in common with the Wizard, with Stilthorn, his grandfather! That doubt and fear and what she told him he wanted should keep him from remembering it!

"I know what is in my blood and hers! Our grandfather's blood!" he cried. "Stilthorn, the great Wizard! His isn't yours! Stilthorn's power and the power of the Women of the Nedoman—they are not both yours, but they are Anna's and they are Elylden's and they are mine!"

Eddris was suddenly furious. "You will be mine! She will be mine! She will! She should have been! Mine! By daughter of *mine*! I will have her when I divide you. When your lives are all a mockery of guile and hypocrisy, of treachery and greed as it is among men, then you will fall! You will all be mine or I will see to it that you die as I saw to it that the mother of your Anna died! As Anna should have died—as one day soon she will! As moment by moment Stilthorn dies! Stilthorn!" she cried, and her voice suddenly changed to a wail. "Stilthorn! To give your life for two wretched mortal children! Stilthorn! Do you hear me? I am Eddris!"

With her outburst of raging words and the final cry of the name of the Wizard, an understanding opened to Keld that left him shattered. Eddris, who wanted both the power of the Wizards and that of the Women of the Nedoman— Eddris had tried to destroy Anna. Eddris, who had taken the place of Anna's mother among the Women of the Nedoman. Anna's mother, the wife of Stilthorn—the incredibly beautiful . . . Eddris had taken her life!

Eddris had wanted to be the wife of Stilthorn!

Had she . . . loved him?

What kind of love would take from him what he had loved most!

Yes, she was beautiful. She was everything. To leave him alone . . .

Love turned to such destruction! *The best thing wrongly used can become the worst!* No! She didn't love him! It was only herself that she loved!

But Stilthorn, had he given his life for . . . ?

It was more than he wanted to understand, more than he wanted to know! He would have to be Stilthorn to understand such things! His eyes burned. The heaviness of the sword was so great that the point fell to the ground.

"Throw it down!" she cried. "That useless sword!"

But using both hands Keld raised it once more. He wanted nothing but to drive her from his sight.

He mounted the slab of rock slowly, cautiously, a step at a time. Struggling to keep the sword before him, watching her always, sick from what he did not want to know but knew, he made his way until he was opposite her on the high edge of a scarp.

"I hate what you are," he whispered. "I hate every part of it. But I am sorry for what you have."

"Sorry! For what?"

"To have—to live—forever—so empty!"

Something must have showed in his face that she could not bear.

"My golden band!" she screamed. "The golden band of my power fills me! I will return to the Valley of the Nedoman for it! And you . . ." With a sweep of her arm she drew his eyes away from her face toward what lay beyond.

It was an abyss so deep it was shrouded in midnight darkness. Beyond it rose mountains, snow-covered, jagged peaks of insurmountable height. Night rushed over the sky with stars whirling close, falling upon him. The ground turned under him and Eddris rushed toward him.

With a cry of terror, Keld stepped back, lifted the sword high with both hands, and swung it to keep her from him. At that instant his arm was struck such a blow that the sword flew from his grasp. It flashed against the sky, a fiery arc, to fall and fall—and vanish. A clawed hand bit into his shoulder. He was dragged backward. The stars of the sky and the darkness of the abyss engulfed him.

38

His head was throbbing, his mouth dry, and he was numb with cold. Keld opened his eyes to find himself lying on his back staring up into blueness. Was this the bottom of the abyss? This icy nothingness, this empty frozen blue—was this the Valley of Hune from which he might escape only to die? There was a weight on his chest as heavy as that of the power of Eddris. He closed his eyes in despair and pushed at it. It was soft and warm. It moved. Another push, this time harder. Something pushed back, stepped on him! And then was gone.

He rolled over, got to his hands and knees, and stared into a row of teeth.

"Thosstoe!"

Keld staggered to his feet and looked around himself. Behind the dog rose the slope. Dwarfed by the mountain's peak, amazed by its height and steepness, he wondered how he had crossed it. It had been difficult but still seemed only a few steps before he stood beside Eddris.

Now it looked to rise hundreds of feet above him! His eyes followed the edge, sharp, jagged, and empty.

Where was she? She must be there! She had come toward him! He had swung the sword, lost it, and . . . and what?

He continued to scan the rock, not believing he would not see her, hear her voice. There was no sign of her. Where had she gone?

Do not let her return in your footsteps.

Had she followed him down the slope? Was she near him, waiting close by until he should go down the mountain? She would call to him. He would see her in a moment behind those rocks. That bank of snow.

Where was she hiding? He had no sword!

Again he scanned the slope, the drifts of snow above him. He found no sign of footprints, neither his nor hers.

"Because I left none," he said suddenly. "I fell!"

He put his hand to the side of his head. His hair was in matted clumps, stiff and dried. His head tender. The sleeve of his coat was torn. How was it she had not forced him forward but rather dragged him backward? How had he pulled away from her?

A last time he searched the ridge with his eyes.

"She's gone, Thosstoe! Gone. Gone, gone! I . . . I drove her away!" Suddenly elated, he threw his arms around the dog and hugged him. Then he turned his back on the gray-and-black rock that drew so sharp a line against the blue sky.

"We'll go back! We'll tell them . . ." His elation slipped away. Stilthorn! He must hurry!

Keld clambered around the boulders below the slanted outcropping and looked at the mountainside. It too had grown and spread immense to left and right. He recognized none of it. There were a hundred ways, one looking no different from another—clefts, boulders, drifts of snow, ice floes, rocky places where the snow had been blown clear.

Where was the cave, the overhanging shelf of rock? There was no sign of it, nothing to tell him how he had come here. The sun had leaped to the other side of the sky. For the first time, Keld shivered from the wind biting through his coat, cold, indifferent.

He rubbed his aching arm. "I don't know where we are, Thosstoe," he whispered. "I don't know the way back. I'll never find the cave! And I've lost the sword!" The last shred of joy left him.

Thosstoe stood beside him, his ears pricked forward, his tail wagging slightly. He looked up at the despairing boy and waited.

Finally the dog sat on his foot. Keld put his hand on Thosstoe's head and caressed him. His fingers touched the collar of rope.

"Show me!" he cried taking hold of the leash. "Take me there!"

Thosstoe was on his feet at once, and they started down the mountain.

Thinking only of Stilthorn and Elylden, Keld tried to hurry but could not. Each step was an effort. His head ached. His hands were stiff with cold. His legs trembled with fatigue. He stumbled and fell, losing hold of the rope. Thosstoe waited for him.

Each time he fell, the dog waited. Each time it was harder to make himself go on. Once he staggered to his feet only to catch the toe of his boot on a branch hidden by snow and fall once more. He lay still, his eyes closed, wondering if he could try one more time.

Suddenly he felt the sharp clawed hand grasp his shoulder. Eddris! She *had* followed him down! She was pulling at him, dragging him!

"No!" he cried, twisted, rolled over, and sat up.

But she was not there. Teeth in the shoulder of his jacket, Thosstoe again tugged at him.

"All right! I'm coming!" Wearily the boy got to his feet and twined the short length of rope around his hand.

Dazed, knowing only that he must keep moving, he watched the ground under his feet. His mind dulled, his thoughts came slowly. Thosstoe! The dog! He must keep hold of the rope. Thosstoe.

A sense of the dog's teeth in his arm reminded him of—what was it?

The hand! The clawed hand he had felt on the mountaintop—the *dog* had pulled him back. Not Eddris. *She* wanted me to fall. Thosstoe . . .

Clever dog! Wise Thosstoe! He must have chased

Eddris away! Now he's taking me back. A dog has four legs. They keep him from falling down. I only have two. The great Keld! The great Knight of Ahln! Can't hold a sword. Can't stand on his feet. Can't find his way home!

Home? Anna? Warm. A fire. Her voice. No! Stilthorn! Elylden!

He said their names over, repeated them again, tried to think of how they looked. Elylden pouting. Elylden teasing. Elylden stamping her foot, wanting her way. Elylden crying. He had promised Anna he would take care of her, but Elylden was crying. His sister, Elylden, sitting on the mountainside alone, frightened because he had walked away. Sitting on the street, her fist against her lips. Frightened because he had lost her . . . Loughat. Now at last she was safe. She was with Stilthorn.

Stilthorn? All he could recall of him were his eyes and his voice. "Go, Keld."

He fell, pushed himself to his knees, crawled, pushed himself to his feet. "Go, Keld."

The path was shadowed before he saw the shelf of rock jutting from the mountainside, the snow high above it glowing an orange red from a sun he could no longer see. Clouds turning dark. Stilthorn, Elylden . . .

Sliding down the last steep slope, boy and dog came to the mouth of the cave. Keld dropped the rope and the dog rushed in. He followed.

"Elylden? Stilthorn?"

There was no answer.

A small ring of fire burned, but there was no sign of his sister or of the Wizard. Shaking with cold and fatigue, the boy added wood to the flames and held his hands over the warmth. Had they left him? It was all right. He would sleep.

Thosstoe barked, a hollow sound that gave back no echo. Keld looked up to see the dog trotting toward the back of the cavern. Calling to him to wait, he stumbled after him into the darkness, tripped over him, and felt for the rope.

39

Stilthorn lay on the low bench of stone, his cape half around him, Elylden's coat folded beneath his head. The girl sat cross-legged on the floor beside him, both of her hands covering one of his, her head resting against his arm.

She leaped up as Keld entered the grotto and ran to throw her arms around him. The boy sank to his knees beside the Wizard, closed his eyes, and leaned against the bench.

When Keld woke he knew he had been in some dark and quiet place in the deepest of sleep. Elylden slept on the floor, her head in his lap. Looking up he found the Wizard's eyes upon him. Stilthorn's face was pale. His lips moved.

"You must leave me now, you and Elylden. We must say good-bye."

Keld drew a deep breath. "No."

Elylden sat up and looked from one to the other.

"It is better that you do—at once," the Wizard said. "Return to the road leading west. You will meet those who flee the fires of both Adnor and the Fane of Monancien.

"Your friend Feirek . . . made a vow. The sword of his poetry has convinced others. They are seeking you—the boy with the ring and his sister. Join them. You have other friends among them. They want a new place to live. A beginning . . . Hold them close. Continue to the west until . . ."

"No!" Elylden cried. "We won't!"

"You must."

"We can't," Keld said. "It's night. We'd lose our way."

The Wizard frowned. "I would not have you . . ." He could not finish the sentence. After a time he murmured, "Tell me how you know she's gone."

"She stood on the ridge of the mountain, the very top. When I looked again, she was gone. I . . . I lost the sword." Keld looked at his hands, at his ring. "It was too heavy. When I lifted it against her, something . . . All I can think of is how it felt when Werfyl kicked me."

"The sword was struck from your hands? Then you stood on the top of the scarp?"

"Yes."

"Monancien warned you, and my last words to you—yet you stood at the edge of the Valley of Hune? But you didn't look into it!"

Keld closed his eyes. The abyss, the gleaming sky, the

jagged mountains, the earth turning under him. The stars falling upon him. Again he felt the awe and the terror.

"I didn't hear you say . . . She was talking. I had to follow her!"

"And she stood with her back to the abyss, while you . . ."

"Yes."

The Wizard shuddered. "What protected you?" he whispered.

"Thosstoe pulled me back."

"He followed you!" Elylden cried. "It's why he left! He knew!"

"There must have been something more," Stilthorn murmured. "And the sword itself—in return for . . . what? Tell me how . . ." He caught his breath.

Keld took his hand. He could not bear to see the Wizard so.

"Tell me all," the Wizard whispered.

All that she said and what he had thought and answered the boy told him haltingly, pausing now and again when he could tell from the tightening grip of his hand that an even greater wave of pain passed through the Wizard, not pain alone but a battle he fought each time. Each time he battled longer. Each time he lost. Each time, though more exhausted, his face a shade paler, he questioned Keld.

"The sword, if I'd held it tighter . . . !"

"The sword of Benelf served you. It is better for everyone that it be where it has gone. You still have the ring?"

Keld nodded and held up his hand.

"Wear it when you shape clay." Stilthorn closed his eyes. They waited. "And then?"

"I thought it was Eddris who took hold of me," the youth told him, "that she was pulling me into the chasm. It looked to be without end, so deep I knew I would fall forever. I thought I would never see you and Elylden again.

"But it wasn't Eddris." He looked down at the white knuckles of his hand that held that of the Wizard and then blurted, "The Valley of Hune—I didn't know until I looked into it that it was there! But Thosstoe did! A dog! He pulled me back. He pulled me—or stopped me from falling, I don't know which. After that, I didn't know my way down the mountain. He brought me here! The dog knew more than I did! I . . . I keep wondering, did I follow her or did I drive her? She was gone, but did I do it or was it Thosstoe who chased her away?"

The Wizard closed his eyes for a moment, then fixed Keld with his dark look. "Did the dog wear the ring and carry the sword for you? Did he run ahead of you and chase her, growl, and worry her skirts? Did he listen to and answer her words?"

"No."

"Then think! Know that no dog can chase evil from a man! He was being a dog, doing what he must. Why do you question what you have done?"

"She told me I followed! When I saw it—where we

were—I thought she led me where she wanted to go! To the Valley of Hune! It must be where she went—back to that valley, and on to the Valley of the Nedoman, back to her power!"

"There is only one way to the Valley of Hune, and it is not that. She had no desire to stand on that mountaintop. She did not follow you back or she would be here now. She will never renew the power she once had. She will never return to the Valley of the Nedoman. She is gone from that world.

"But understand, Keld, even now she is finding her way down the mountain. She will walk . . . in your world for the rest of time. Remember her face. Remember that she is merciless.

"Son of Anna, you walked against her this time. Remember that, for you will have to do it . . . again and again. Know that you have the strength, even without the sword of Benelf.

"You must show it can be done, and the knowledge of that must be kept alive. For your children and their children . . . will have to walk against her."

When he spoke again his voice was even more halting.

"Men forget what she is . . . for that is the way of it here. Perhaps because they do not live long. Each child born, begins from the . . . beginning. The lessons of the past are forgotten . . . The simplest lesson that kindness breeds kindness, love breeds love . . . and hate breeds hate.

"The learned . . . the Monanciens . . . grow wise and

then . . . too old. Thinking all are like themselves, they put faith in the brothers Graphuys . . . the small of mind . . . the selfish . . . Arrogance, suspicion, and finally hatred . . . and soon the opposites rule. The brutal, the hungry for power . . . the Blygens . . . with Eddris standing beside them."

He closed his eyes. Opened them.

"Man, divided, always of opposites. Joy and grief, kindness and cruelty, love and hate . . . How he struggles with himself! Too much of the Valley of the Nedoman has faded from here since we left.

"You have it in you to bring some of it back to your world, children of Anna. This one lesson . . . that until all children are reared . . . with the oneness of love for one another . . . man will suffer . . . forever."

Once more the Wizard battled. He was silent for a long time before he asked in a whisper, "Did you see mountains against the night sky?" There was a moment of longing on his face.

"Oh, yes! Sharp peaks covered with snow! Far higher than those behind the Crags of Ahln! Covering the sky! Reaching to the stars! Like nothing else!"

"Yes, like nothing else! And if you should climb them, Keld, you would find . . . higher ones beyond."

They waited. Elylden put both her hands against his face.

"There is comfort in your touch, Elylden," he whispered. "Hands that heal . . . Anna . . . Anna is learning from her mother . . . Anna will wake them . . ." Keld, holding his hand, knew the battle was greater still.

When Stilthorn opened his eyes, it was to look at the statue. "For the only time in my life, I am grateful for her death. She died quickly, with no pain. It was an accident."

Keld opened his mouth to cry out the truth but clamped his lips shut against the words and turned his face aside.

"Keld, you suffer every man's pain too much. Watch that it not become a fault. Compassion calls for . . . strength. It requires you to take action. You cannot stand by and weep and wring your hands, simply suffer the . . . anguish of others without . . . bringing . . . justice, hope. Remember my words! Let them . . . drive you. Do what must be done. Never doubt . . . yourself." He closed his eyes. When he opened them it was to look again upon the statue, as if each time it gave him an instant's respite, the faintest breath of strength.

Keld's eyes followed his. The statue, so beautiful, so alive! So still. If only it could breathe, could speak!

Elylden too stared at the statue. Her eyes widened, her lips parted. Slowly she rose to her feet and crossed to it. She stood before it, gazing up at the face. She stood on tiptoe. Slowly she reached up to touch the out-stretched hand.

Astounded, Keld saw her lift from it a golden circlet.

She turned her face to him, a look in her eyes he had never seen. A look of wonder. Awed, frightened beyond tears, resolute. She returned to Stilthorn's side. Kneeling beside him, she pressed the ring into his hand and folded his fingers over it, holding them tightly with her own.

The Wizard grew quiet. He scarcely breathed. When he opened his eyes at last, there was no pain in them.

"Is it finished then?" he murmured. "So soon? But I still . . ."

Keld and Elylden bent over him. His face showed disbelief at the sight of them. "You cannot have come with me!"

"No," Elylden whispered. Her own eyes were wide and shining. "You told me that this circlet was her knowledge of healing. That . . . Now you'll live! You can stay with us!"

"The circlet? From the hand of . . ." He glanced toward the statue and was amazed as neither of them had ever seen him. He lifted his hand and opened his fingers to gaze at the delicate ring of gold that lay in his palm. "Might it have been given for the sword?"

Then he whispered, "There is more power in your hands than fire, Elylden. You must learn with greatest care to use it all. One day you will give your gifts to your daughter as they were given you by Anna. Not only Sirdde walks on this poor earth!" He shook his head. "No, I cannot go with you. The ring cannot do that. But it has taken away the pain so that I shall sleep quietly— and soon."

For a moment he was silent, then asked, "You have a question, Keld?"

"The Knights of Ahln . . . Should I seek them now?"

The Wizard was silent for a long time before answering. "No, don't seek them. They take separate ways.

Now and then, in a time of great need, a Knight of Ahln will come—a man among men. In your life one may come to you. Perhaps more. They know what you have done. And you—you have more of Anna within you than you know or you never would have seen them. You know what they are—their courage, their truth to themselves. Seek it in those close to you. Ask it of them. Demand it of yourself.

"To battle Eddris . . . perhaps Fel . . . That is all I can tell you."

His eyes went again to the girl. "Take the circlet, Elylden." He pushed it gently into her hand. "Return it to her. I no longer need it. Take your coat from beneath my head. You'll want it against the cold. Keld, take up the edges of my cape. Wrap it more tightly around me. Wait!" He lifted his hand and touched their faces, first Elylden's and then Keld's, as Anna had always done. "Draw my cowl up, Elylden, over my eyes. Now . . . you must go . . ." His voice faded to a breath of a whisper. ". . . quickly."

His look went far beyond them and then his eyes closed.

They knelt side by side. The room grew more and more silent.

"Stilthorn?" Elylden asked in a small voice. And then she began to cry.

Keld put his arms around her, his own tears hot and stinging.

At last he turned from the Wizard's stillness to gaze at

the statue. The outstretched arm and hand empty of its golden ring seemed now a gracious gesture of welcome.

For Stilthorn? His eyes blurred again.

"We have to go, Elylden. We have to leave him here."

Her head moved against his shoulder and they stood up. Elylden drew the cowl over Stilthorn's forehead and eyes.

Keld took up a lamp. "He said to go quickly."

"We'll leave the other light," Elylden told him.

Hand in hand they descended the stairs. Thosstoe rose and trotted ahead of them. A little way and they stopped to look back at the bright shaft from the single lamp.

"It will never go out," Elylden whispered.

Suddenly Keld remembered. "Elylden, you didn't put it back in her hand! You can't have it. Take it back!"

"I don't have it. I left it with Stilthorn. Under the cowl."

They lingered. How quiet it was, the gentle light, the still air around them, the deepening of the silence. So deep that it became more than stillness, thicker than the air, darker than the darkness, heavier than the mountain. They felt it, a gathering of force within the quiet, a slipping over them like the breath of a touch not felt, of the certainty of a storm building beyond some distant horizon, not seen, not heard, but there, and known.

There was a sudden loud crack, and then another. The ground shook. A mass of rock within the mountain, split from high above, fell with a roar. The light behind them was gone.

Sand and small stones showered down upon Keld and his sister. Holding hands, they ran, Thosstoe loping ahead of them. There was a second clap like that of thunder that comes with the very instant of lightning. They were thrown to the ground with the shaking, and the mountain rumbled behind them. The lamp went out.

Keld dragged Elylden to her feet. Ahead of them shone the tiny point of fire. On they ran, a pale light from the mouth of the cavern growing. Once more the ground trembled before they came breathless to the wide cavern.

Keld freed the rearing horses, and with a quick slap for each, drove them into the dawn. He snatched up their small bundles.

Elylden, dropping to her knees, stopped to feed the circle of fire.

"Don't! There's no time!" Keld cried, pulling at her.

But Elylden, a small log in each hand, pushed him away and laid the wood carefully on the embers, then set a third across the other two. She scrambled to her feet, and, backing toward the entrance, paused, shook her hand with a quick snap, and stretched it toward the smoking embers. A blaze of white fire flared up, a dazzling light, a slender column of fierce brilliance.

"It will never go out!" she cried as Keld grasped her arm and pulled her from the cave.

40

The snow was heavy and wet, the day warm. Small rivulets ran down the faces of boulders. Banks of snow slipped suddenly away from their path to fall to the rocks below. The horses chose their way carefully. The dog trotted ahead.

They came upon a bare shoulder of mountain, where no tree had put down roots. Thosstoe stopped to lap water from a small pool and scratch his back in a plot of brown grass. Deciding it was to his liking, he stopped in the middle of the rolling and dozed with his legs in the air.

Keld and Elylden dismounted. This place they had stopped when the Wizard had first told them of the cavern. *A place of rest.*

Keld's eyes burned. Elylden stood forlorn. Stilthorn's presence was everywhere—in the rocks, the snow, the wind, an eagle soaring—his voice in every place they knew he would stop to point out the beauty. His boundless love for the lakes and rivers, meadows and mountains and for the creatures that lived in them embraced all that lay before them. His absence was a hollow universe.

They looked back and up. The shelf of rock jutted out, the dark shadow beneath it, above it a steep wall of snow.

"Why didn't it heal him?" Elylden asked.

"It stopped his pain. How could he have borne any worse?"

Stilthorn . . . Was the lamp still burning? Whoever entered the cavern would never find the small grotto. Keld could not take his eyes from the opening.

While they watched, the wind struck them, biting cold and clean. A puff of white whirled out from the top of the high bank of snow above the cave. Then another. A cloud of snow whipped from the length of it. Suddenly the whole began to slip, hundreds of feet of it above the shelf. Faster and faster it went, a frothing mass not only of snow but of boulders, rock, and gravel. Down it came like the white water of the falls of Gresheen, tumbling with clouds of icy mist swirling into the air. On down it went below the cave, another mass of sliding snow, trees, and boulders. Then came the sound, the rumble and the roar of it setting off lesser falls of snow on lower slopes.

When the air cleared of spray and rock and sound, the shelf had vanished. The entrance to the cave had disappeared, sealed by a wide slab of stone. Below it, the mountainside had been sheared away, the polished gorge of rock falling a thousand feet.

There was no path to the cave, no entrance to it, no trace of what had been.

"It's gone! All of it!" Keld whispered.

"No." Elylden too spoke in a whisper. "Not the cavern. Not Stilthorn. Only the *way* to the Valley of Hune from here is gone."

"He said it wasn't that way." Keld lifted his eyes to the dark peak. Where had he stood looking down into that feared valley?

"Not over the mountain. *Through* it. I asked him. It was the way Anna went. It was the way your father went to find her. No one will ever find the way from here again."

"The way to forever . . . is gone."

"No." Elylden's lips scarcely moving, she murmured, "Fire and the wind, rock and the sea. Remember the old ones? *They* are forever."

They are forever for something that I can never tell even Keld of, she thought. She saw Stilthorn scoop a shallow grave in the dirt. Saw the Wizard push the golden band into it and bury it. Watched him kindle the fire above it and heard his command.

"It must never go out."

Fire, wind, snow, the side of the mountain . . . would Eddris ever find it? "Never. I hope never," she whispered.

Each place they had stopped, Stilthorn had provided for them.

Before they came to the shepherd's cottage, Elylden said defiantly, "His knowledge was not taken from him. He spoke to us wisely before he slept. His power was not taken from him. He brought down the mountain twice even while he slept! His life could not have been taken from him. He needs rest, but he will waken."

Keld shook his head. "Oh, Elylden! If I could believe that!"

When her silence grew long and he saw the pout set on her lips, he reminded her gently. "Remember what Monancien said. *Do not mix what is with what you imagine.*"

Her scowl deepened. "Monancien was Monancien. Stilthorn is Stilthorn."

Keld sighed. For him the door had closed forever. But for Elylden? She was still pouting. He frowned. Perhaps Eddris was right. What did he know of his sister? Not everything.

Winter storms swept the country, and there were days they could not travel. Again the Wizard had provided for them for they were welcomed in every house or inn they came to for however long they must wait for the weather to be kind.

In the spring they came to a hill and looked upon the road lying close below them. There, strung along the way that wound through a gentle valley, were wagons and carts, folk on horses, folk on donkeys, folk on foot. Cows and goats ambled behind, dogs running among them.

As they came closer . . .

"Look! I think—yes! It's Feirek and Toseny! I see . . . There's . . . And Arela! What Stilthorn told us—people of Adnor! They're looking for a better place, a better way!"

"They're looking for *us*!" Elylden exclaimed. "We'll go with them to find it! One that's safe for the books Stilthorn said they saved!"

"I'll build a library. We'll add ours to theirs!"

"We don't have any!"

"Oh yes we do! Not written down—not yet. But we know them! The words and songs of Anna, the histories of the old ones, and of the giants, of the time of the wise ones, of Benelf of the Hundreds and the journey of the Wizards and the Women of the Nedoman and the Knights of Ahln to the Valley of the Nedoman. And of Anna herself and of . . ."

Elylden waited long before asking him to finish telling her.

"Of Stilthorn," he whispered, "and the golden band of Eddris."

EPILOGUE

With the help of Brother Quinolur and two scribes from the Fane of Monancien, Toseny kept a careful history of the people and their journey from Adnor to the sea.

There were happenings that he did not know of. These Elylden kept in her journal:

Scroot—whoever's dice he threw came up a four and a six.

A forest they passed through she found to hold Stilthorn's powers. She called it Wood of No-name, so that what dwelt there would never be disturbed while he slept.

She stood with her brother on a high cliff and looked at what lay below. The brown rounded hills, the sea . . .
"It's the Plain of Tregaed!" she said. "Just as Anna told us!"

When she looked at Keld, she saw that he had grown pale.

"I know," he said. "I've been here."

They walked upon the shore.

"Fel vowed that he would never again do battle here. I'll build a castle—with the library. There." Keld pointed to a wall of stone, the base of an ancient ruin.

Elylden asked, "How can you build it in such a steep, jagged, rocky place?"

Keld said, "With my hands."

There was a moment even Elylden did not know of:

It was an evening at sunset when Keld stood on the ancient stone wall and looked at the sea, the library rising behind him. They had asked him to be king. Was he worthy? Should he say yes or no?

He saw them then—shadows, transparent, like reflections in a window of glass in the Fane of Monancien, riders, tall knights. Two score, perhaps, they moved northward along the shore, faded and were gone. Another rider came, the horse splashing through running foam, hooves pocking the sand as it turned from the sea toward the fortress.

Drawing near, the youth lifted his face toward Keld and raised his spear to wave a greeting. No longer that of a small boy, thin, pale, the eyes pleading, yearning, hopeful and hopeless at the same time, the face was strong, eager, assured.

Ask it of them, Stilthorn had said.

"As I have been asked to . . ."

Demand it of yourself.

"Why not?" Keld murmured as he waved an arm to acknowledge the greeting. "Why not."